By the Good Sainte Anne

A Story of Modern Quebec

Anna Chapin Ray

Alpha Editions

This edition published in 2022

ISBN : 9789356154384

Design and Setting By
Alpha Editions
www.alphaedis.com
Email - info@alphaedis.com

As per information held with us this book is in Public Domain.
This book is a reproduction of an important historical work. Alpha Editions uses the best technology to reproduce historical work in the same manner it was first published to preserve its original nature. Any marks or number seen are left intentionally to preserve its true form.

Contents

CHAPTER ONE ....- 1 -
CHAPTER TWO ....- 8 -
CHAPTER THREE ....- 13 -
CHAPTER FOUR...- 19 -
CHAPTER FIVE ....- 25 -
CHAPTER SIX...- 29 -
CHAPTER SEVEN ....- 35 -
CHAPTER EIGHT ....- 41 -
CHAPTER NINE..- 47 -
CHAPTER TEN..- 54 -
CHAPTER ELEVEN..- 62 -
CHAPTER TWELVE...- 69 -
CHAPTER THIRTEEN..- 77 -
CHAPTER FOURTEEN ....- 84 -
CHAPTER FIFTEEN ....- 91 -
CHAPTER SIXTEEN...- 100 -
CHAPTER SEVENTEEN ....- 107 -
CHAPTER EIGHTEEN..- 113 -
CHAPTER NINETEEN..- 120 -
CHAPTER TWENTY ....- 127 -
CHAPTER TWENTY-ONE..- 135 -
CHAPTER TWENTY-TWO...- 140 -
CHAPTER TWENTY-THREE ....- 146 -

CHAPTER ONE

Petulantly Nancy Howard cast aside her letter and buried her chin in her cupped palms.

"Oh, the woes of having a learned father!" she sighed. "Here is Joe's letter, telling me how everything is starting up at home; and here am I, Nancy Howard, buried in this picturesque, polyglot wilderness, just because my sire feels himself moved to take a vacation from medicine in order to study history at first hand! I wish he would let his stupid monograph go to the winds, and take me home in time for the Leighton's dinner, next week."

She picked up the scattered sheets of her letter and ran them over once more, holding up her left hand, as she did so, to cut off the dazzling sunshine from the white paper. It was a pretty hand, slim, strong and tapering. Prettier still was her head, erect and crowned with piles of reddish-brown hair. It was not without apparent reason that Nancy Howard had been, for the past year, one of the most popular girls of her social circle at home.

At the third page, her brows wrinkled thoughtfully. Dropping the loose sheets into her lap, she once more fell to musing aloud.

"It does seem to me that Joe is seeing a good deal of Persis Routh. I never thought he liked her especially well. But anyway I am out of all the fun. Space isn't the only thing that makes distance. Up here, I am at least two hundred years away from home. How long have I been here? Eight, no, nine days." Suddenly she laughed. "At least, it has been a period of fasting and meditation. I believe I'll count it as a novena to the Good Sainte Anne. Perhaps she will manufacture a miracle in my behalf, and get up a little excitement for me. Fancy an excitement in this place!"

"B'jour, mam'selle."

Nancy turned alertly, as the voice broke in upon her musings.

"Bon jour, madame," she answered, with a painstaking French which laid careful stress upon each silent letter and separated the words into an equal number of distinct sentences. At present, it was her latest linguistic accomplishment, and she aired it with manifest pride.

Pausing midway over the stile, the old woman brushed her face with the apron that hung above her tucked-up skirt.

"Why not you go to the church?" she asked.

Nancy breathed a sigh of relief, as the talk lapsed into her mother tongue. Like most Americans, she preferred that conversational eccentricities should be entirely upon the other side, and she questioned how far she could go upon the strength of her own three words. Nevertheless, she framed her reply on the idioms of her companion.

"Why for should I go?"

The woman set down her pail of water on the top step of the stile. Then she planted herself just below it, with her coarse boots resting on the crisp brown turf.

"We go to church, all the days," she admonished Nancy sternly.

The girl smiled irrepressibly.

"So I have noticed," she said, half under her breath. Then she added hastily, "But we do not."

"Are you Catholique?"

Nancy shook her head.

"Too bad! But surely you can pray in any church."

This time, Nancy felt a rebuke.

"Yes," she assented; "but I am not used to going, every day."

"No. No?" The second *no* was plainly interrogative. "But the Good Sainte Anne only does those miracle to them that pray without ceasing."

The girl faced about sharply.

"Madame Gagnier, have you ever seen a miracle?"

The wide flat hat nodded assent.

"A real, true miracle?"

"Yes, so many."

"Hh! I'd like to see one."

Two keen old eyes peered up at her from beneath the wide hat.

"Mam'selle does not believe?"

There was reproach in the accent; but the girl answered undauntedly,—

"Not one bit. I'll wait till I have seen one."

Madame Gagnier shrugged her shoulders ever so slightly.

"How shall you see, having no eyes at all?"

Nancy's brown eyes snapped in defiant contradiction of the slight put upon them. It was no part of her plan to be drawn into theological discussion.

However, theological discussion being forced upon her, she had no mind to give way. Motherless from her childhood, Nancy Howard had never been trained in the purely feminine grace of suppressing her opinions.

"I not only have eyes; but I have a little common sense," she answered aggressively.

The next instant, she was conscious of a sudden wave of contrition. Madame Gagnier unclasped her wrinkled hands and crossed herself devoutly.

"Then may the Good Sainte Anne open your eyes!" she responded, with gentle simplicity. "You carry her name. Pray that she take you under her protection, and work this miracle in your behalf. She is all-gracious, and her goodness has not any limits at all."

Impulsively the girl rose from her seat on the ground, crossed to the stile and dropped down on its lowest step.

"Madame Gagnier, I was very rude," she said, with equal simplicity.

Then silence dropped over them, the silence of the country and of the past. Forgetful of the letter she had let slip to the ground, forgetful of the coarse, mannish boots beside her own dainty ties, the girl allowed her gaze to wander back and forth across the view. It had grown so familiar to her during the last nine days, interminable days to the energetic, society-loving American girl who had chafed at her exile from the early gayeties of the awakening season in town.

Fifty feet away stood her temporary prison, a long, narrow stone house coated with shining white plaster. Above its single story, the pointed roof shot up sharply, broken by two dormer windows and topped with a chimney at either end, the one of stone, the other of brick. The palings in front of the house were white, dotted with their dark green posts; but, the house once passed, the neat palings promptly degenerated into a post-and-rail fence guiltless of paint and crossed with a stile at important strategic points connected with the barn. For one hundred feet in front of the house, the smooth-cropped lawn rolled gently downward. Then it dropped sharply from the crest of the bluff in an almost perpendicular grassy wall reaching down to the single long street of Beaupré, two hundred feet below. The crest of the bluff was dotted by an occasional farmhouse, each reached by its zigzag trail up the slope; but, in the street beneath, the houses met in two continuous, unbroken lines, parallel to that other continuous line of the mighty river. The river was mud-colored, to-day; and the turf about her was browned by early frosts; but the Isle of Orleans lay blue in the middle distance, and, far to the north, Cap Tourmente rested in a purple haze. At her feet, the white sail of a stray fishing-boat caught the sunlight and tossed it back to her, and, nearer still, the gray twin spires of Sainte Anne-de-Beaupré rose in the clear October air.

"Mother of the Holy Virgin, protector of sailors, healer of the faithful, patron saint of the New France." Dame Gagnier was rehearsing the attributes of the saint to herself in her own harsh *patois*.

The girl interrupted her ruthlessly.

"What an enormous train!" she exclaimed.

"Eh?"

Nancy pointed to the long line of cars crawling up to the station beside the church.

"Long train. Many cars," she explained slowly.

Dame Gagnier's eyes followed the pointing finger.

"Yes. It is a pilgrimage," she answered.

The girl scrambled to her feet.

"Really? A pilgrimage! I thought it was too late in the season. Do you suppose there will be a miracle?" she questioned eagerly.

Under the wide hat, the eyes lighted and the wrinkled lips puckered into a smile.

"Mam'selle does not believe in those miracle," Madame Gagnier reminded her.

Nancy's shoulders shaped themselves into an American travesty of the inimitable French shrug.

"I am always open to conviction," she announced calmly.

"Eh?"

"I am going to see for myself."

"Mam'selle will go to church?"

"Yes; that is, if you are sure it is a pilgrimage."

"What else?" In her turn, Madame Gagnier pointed to the train whence a stream of humanity was pouring into the square courtyard of the Basilica.

"You are sure? I don't want to break my neck for nothing, scrambling down your ancestral driveway."

"Eh?"

For the thousandth time during the past nine days, Nancy felt an unreasoning rage against the deliberate monosyllable that checked her whimsical talk. In time, it becomes annoying to be obliged to explain all one's figures of speech. Abruptly she pulled herself up and began again.

"Unless you are sure it is a pilgrimage, I do not wish to walk down the steep slope," she amended.

"Yes. It is a pilgrimage from Lake Saint John. My son told me. It is the last pilgrimage of the year."

Nancy clasped her hands in rapture.

"Glory be!" she breathed fervently. "I am in great luck, to-day, for they said that it was too late in the year to expect any more of them. The Good Sainte Anne is working in my behalf. Now, if she will only produce a miracle, I'll be quite content. Good by, Madame Gagnier!"

Madame Gagnier nodded, as she looked after the alert, erect figure.

"Mam'selle does not believe in those miracle," she said calmly. "Well, she shall see."

The girl stooped to pick up her letters. Then swiftly she crossed the lawn and entered the house. Outside a closed door, she paused and tapped softly.

"Come in." The answering voice was impersonal, abstracted.

Pushing open the door, Nancy entered the little sitting-room and crossed to the desk by the sunny window looking out on the river.

"Daddy dear, are you going to come with me, for an hour or two?"

The figure before the desk lost its scholarly abstraction and came back to the present. The student of antiquity had changed to the adoring father of a most modern sort of American girl; and his eyes, leaving the musty ecclesiastical records, brightened with a wholly worldly pride in his pretty daughter.

"What now?"

"A pilgrimage. A great, big pilgrimage, the last one of the year," she said eagerly. "I'm going down to see it. Surely you'll go, too."

He shook his head.

"Oh, do," she urged. "You ought to see it, as a matter of history. It is worth more than tons of old records, this seeing middle-age miracles happening in these prosy modern days."

"Sainte Anne-de-Beaupré isn't Lourdes, Nancy," he cautioned her.

"No; but the guide-books say it is only second to Lourdes," she answered undauntedly. "Anyway, I want to see what is happening. Won't you come, really, daddy?"

His eyes twinkled, as they looked up into her animated face.

"Nancy, I am sixty-five years old, and that trail up the hill is worse than the Matterhorn. If you follow the zigzags, you walk ten miles in order to accomplish one hundred feet; if you strike out across country, you have to wriggle up on all fours. I know, for I have tried it. It isn't a seemly thing for a man of my years to come crawling home, flat on his stomach."

She laughed, as she stood drumming idly on the table.

"I am sorry. It is so much more fun to have somebody to play with. Still, I shall go, even if I must go alone."

She started towards the door; then turned to face him, as he added hastily,—

"And, if you see Père Félicien, ask him when I can examine those last records by Monseigneur Laval. I shall be here, tell him, about ten days longer."

Nancy's face fell.

"Ten mortal days! Oh, daddy!"

"Yes, I shall need as much time as that. I prefer to finish up my work here, before I go on to Quebec."

"And how long do you mean to stay in Quebec?" she asked.

The minor cadence in her tone escaped her father's ears. He patted the papers before him caressingly.

"It is impossible to tell. Four or five weeks, I should say. That ought to give me time to gather my materials."

Nancy loved her gay home life; but she also loved her father. She tossed him a kiss as she left the room; nevertheless, the smile that accompanied the kiss was rather forlorn and wavering. Once outside the door, however, she freed her mind.

"Ten more days here, and a month in that hole of a Quebec! It will be Thanksgiving, before we get home. Think of all the fun I shall be losing!" She pinned on her hat with a series of energetic pries and pushes. Then she added fervently, "Oh, Good Sainte Anne, do get up the greatest miracle of all, and produce something or somebody that shall add a little variety to my existence! I'll give fifty cents to the souls in purgatory, if you'll only be good enough to rescue my soul from this absolute boredom of boredoms."

Surely, never was more unorthodox prayer directed upward from any shrine. However, the Good Sainte Anne chanced to be in a propitious mood, that day.

CHAPTER TWO

Mr. Cecil Barth was unfeignedly low in his mind, that morning. The causes were various and sundry.

First of all, Quebec was a bore. In the second place, the only people to whom he had brought letters of introduction had most inconsiderately migrated to Vancouver, and, fresh from his English university, he was facing the prospect of a solitary winter before he could go out into ranch life in the spring. A Britisher of sorts, it had not appeared to him to be necessary to inform himself in advance regarding the conditions, climatic and social, of the new country to which he was going. Now, too late, he recognized his mistake. A third grievance lay in the non-arrival of the English mail, that morning; and the fourth and most fatal of all lurked in the kindly efforts of his table companion to draw him into the conversation. To his mind, there was no reason that the swarthy, black-browed little Frenchman at his elbow should offer him any comments upon the state of the weather. The Frenchman had promptly retired from the talk; but his dark eyes had lighted mirthfully, as they had met the asphalt-like stare of his neighbor's eyeglasses. Adolphe St. Jacques possessed his own fair share of a sense of humor; and Cecil Barth was a new element in his experience.

"Monsieur has swallowed something stiff that does not agree with him," he observed blandly to his fellow student across the table; and Barth, whose French was of Paris, not of Canada, was totally at a loss to account for their merriment.

For the past week, the group of students and the chatter of their Canadian *patois* had been anathema to him. He understood not a word of their talk, and consequently, with the extreme sensitiveness which too often accompanies extreme egotism, he imagined that it related solely to himself. In vain he tried to avoid their hours for meals. Rising betimes, he met them at the hurried early breakfast which betokened an eight o'clock lecture. The next morning, dreary loitering in his room only brought him into the midst of the deliberate meal which was the joyous prerogative of their more leisurely days. Barth liked The Maple Leaf absolutely; but he hated the students of his own table with a cordial and perfect hatred.

Dropped from the Allan Line steamer, one bright September morning, as a matter of course he had been driven up through the gray old town to the Chateau Frontenac. A week at the Chateau had been quite enough for him. To his mind, its luxurious rooms had been altogether too American. Too American, also, were its inhabitants. He shrank from the obvious brides in their new tailor gowns and their evident absorption in their companions. He resented those others who, more elderly or more detached, roused themselves from their absorption to bestow a friendly word on the solitary young Englishman. Their clothes, their accent, and, worst of all, their manners betrayed their alien birth. No self-respecting woman, bride or no bride, ever wore such dainty shoes. No man of education ever stigmatized an innocent babe as *cunning*. And there was no, absolutely no, excuse for the familiar greetings bestowed upon himself by complete strangers.

"Americans!" quoth Mr. Cecil Barth. "Oh, rather!"

And, next morning, he went in search of another hostelry.

He found it at The Maple Leaf, just across the Place d'Armes. Fate denied to him the privilege of sleeping in the quaint little *pension* whose roof was sanctified by having once sheltered his compatriot, Dickens; he could only take his meals there, and hunt for a room outside. At noon, he came to dinner, too exhausted by his fruitless search to care whether or not the students were at the table, or on it, or even under it. Go back to the Chateau he would not; but he began to fear lest the only alternative lay in a tent pitched on the terrace in the lee of the Citadel and, in that wilderness, he questioned whether anything so modern as a tent could be bought.

After dinner, the Lady of The Maple Leaf took his affairs in hand. She possessed the two essentials, a kindly heart and a sense of humor. She had seen stray Britishers before; she had a keen perception of the artistic fitness of things and, by twilight, Mr. Cecil Barth was sitting impotently upon his boxes in the third-floor front room of the town house of the Duke of Kent. He had very little notion of the way to proceed about unpacking himself. Nevertheless, as he put on his glasses and stared at the panelled shutters of his ducal casement, he felt more at peace with the world than he had done for two long weeks.

In after years, he never saw fit to divulge the details of his unpacking. It accomplished itself chiefly by the simple method of his tossing out on the floor whatever things lay above any desired object, of leaving those things on the floor until he became weary of tangling his feet in them, then of stowing them away in any convenient corner that offered itself. By this simple method, however, he had contrived to gain space enough to permit of his tramping up and down the floor, and it was there that he had been taking petulant exercise, that bright October morning.

At last he halted at the window and stood looking down into the street beneath. The Duke of Kent's house has the distinction, rare in Saint Louis Street, of standing well back within its own grounds, and, from his window, Barth could watch the leisurely procession passing to and fro on the wooden sidewalks which separated the gray stone buildings from the paler gray stripe of asphalt between. Even at that early hour, it was a variegated procession.

Tailor-made girls mingled with black-gowned nuns, soldiers from the Citadel, swaggering jauntily along, jostled a brown-cowled Franciscan friar or a portly citizen with his omnipresent umbrella, while now and then Barth caught sight of a scarlet-barred khaki uniform, or of the white serge robe and dove-colored cloak of a sister from the new convent out on the Grand Allée.

Barth had travelled before; he had seen many cities; nevertheless, he acknowledged the charm of this varied humanity, so long as it remained safely at his feet. Then he glanced diagonally across the road to the Montcalm headquarters, and discovered the patch of sunshine that lay over its pointed gables.

"Jolly sort of day!" he observed to himself. "I believe I'll try to see something or other."

With a swift forgiveness for the past days of scurrying clouds, of the woes of moving, even of students and Americans, he turned away from the window, caught up his hat, stick and gloves, and ran lightly down the staircase. Once out in the street, he strayed past the English cathedral, past the gray old front of the Basilica, turned to his left, then turned again and wandered aimlessly down Palace Hill. Ten minutes later, he stopped beside an electric train and watched the crowd scrambling into its cars.

"Sainte Anne-de-Beaupré," he read from the label in a rear window. "What can be the attraction there? Oh, I know; it's that American Lourdes place. How awfully American to go to its miracles by electricity! I believe I'll go, too. It might be rather interesting to see what an American miracle is like."

Ticket in hand, he boarded the train, already moving out of the station. He had some difficulty in finding a seat to his liking, since a man of finical habits objects to having two bundle-laden habitants in the same seat with himself. However, by the time he was sliding along under the bluff at Beauport, with the Saint Lawrence glistening on his right, he decided that the morning was ideal for a country ride. By the time the train halted opposite the Falls of Montmorency, he had forgotten the ubiquitous students at his table, and, as he entered into the fertile valley of L'Ange Gardien, he came to the conclusion that chance had led him wisely. Just how wisely, as yet he was in ignorance.

It was still long before midday when the train drew up at Sainte Anne station, and Barth stepped out upon the platform. Then in amazement he halted to look about him. Close at hand, an arched gateway led into a broad square garden, bounded by gravel walks and bordered on two sides by a row of little shrines, aged and weatherbeaten. On the third side stood the church of the Good Sainte Anne, its twin gray towers rising sharply against the blue

October sky and flanking the gilded statue of the saint poised on the point of the middle roof. Around the four sides of the courtyard there slowly filed a motley procession of humanity, here a cripple, there one racked by some mental agony, the sick in mind and body, simple-hearted and trusting, each bringing his secret grief to lay at the feet of the Good Sainte Anne. Mass was already over, and the procession had formed again to march to the shrine and to the holy altar.

Barth's eyes roved over the shabby procession, over the faces, dull and heavy, or alert with trust; then he turned to the rose-arched figure borne on the shoulders of the chanting priests, and his blood throbbed in his veins, as he listened to their rich, sonorous voices.

"A pilgrimage!" he ejaculated to himself. "And now for a miracle! May the saint be propitious, for once in a way!"

Following hard on the heels of the crowd, he pushed his way through one of the wide doors, gave a disdainful glance at the huge racks of crutches and braces left by long generations of pious pilgrims, looked up at the vaulted roof, forward to the huge statue of Sainte Anne half-way up the middle aisle, and drew a deep breath of content. The next minute, he choked, as the stifling atmosphere of the place swept into his throat and nostrils.

"Oh, by George!" said Mr. Cecil Barth.

However, once there, he resolved to see the spectacle to the end. Furthermore, Barth was artist to the core of his being, and those sonorous voices, now ringing down from the organ loft above, could atone for much stale air. A step at a time, he edged forward cautiously and took his place not far from the altar rail.

The students of his table would have found it hard to recognize the haughty young Englishman in the man who knelt there, looking with pitiful eyes at the forlorn stream of humanity that flowed past him. Was it all worth while: the weary fastings and masses, the scrimping of tiny incomes for the sake of the journey and of the offering at the shrine, the faith and hope, and the infinite, childlike trust, all to culminate in the moment of kneeling at the carved altar rail, of feeling the sacred relic touched to one's lips and to the plague-spot of body or of soul? And then they were brushed aside with the monotonous brushing of the relic across the folded napkin in the left hand of the priest. For better or worse, the pilgrimage was over. It was the turn of the next man. Brushed aside, he rose from his knees to give place to the next, and yet the next.

Just once the monotony was broken. A worn pair of crutches dropped at the feet of the statue; a worn old man, white to his lips, staggered forward, knelt and received the healing touch on lip and thigh and knee. Then, with every nerve tense, he struggled to his feet and made his toilsome way to the outer world, while the priests recorded one more miracle wrought by the Good Sainte Anne. Then the monotony fell again, and became seemingly interminable.

At length Barth could endure it no longer. Rising impatiently, he forced his way down the crowded aisle and came out into the air once more. After the dim, dark church and the choking cloud of the incense, the rush of sunshiny ozone struck him in the face like a lash, and involuntarily he raised his head and squared his shoulders to meet it. He loitered along the gravel pathway, watching the habitants who, their pious pilgrimage over, were opening their crumpled valises and spreading out their luncheons in the cloisters to the south of the church. Then, tossing a coin into the tin cup of the blind beggar in the gateway, he came out of the court and crossed the road to the little hillside chapel built of the seventeenth-century materials of the old church of Sainte Anne. But the spell of the place was still upon him; in his mind's eye, he yet saw the endless line of pilgrims, bowing and rising in unbroken succession. With unseeing gaze, he stared at the rows of carts heaped with their ecclesiastical trinkets, at the stray figures lifting themselves heavenward by means of the Scala Sancta Chapel, and at the line of white farmhouses poised high on the bluff beyond. Then, yielding to the spell of the kneeling figures, of the incense-filled air and of the chanting voices, he turned and hurried back again to the church.

By the time he reached the steps once more, the procession was flowing swiftly outward, and the little platform at the doorway was crowded with excited figures. Barth tried this door and then that, in a futile endeavor to regain his old place near the altar rail; but again and again he was forced backward to the very verge of the steps. Then an unduly tall habitant elbowed Barth's glasses from his nose. He bent down to pick them up, was jostled rudely from behind, lost his balance and rolled down the steps where he landed in a dusty, ignominious heap in the midst of a knot of women.

During one swift second, it seemed to Barth that the vast statue of Sainte Anne had tumbled from the roof, to dazzle his eyes with her gilding and to crush his body with her weight. Then the dancing lights and the shooting pains ended in darkness and peace.

CHAPTER THREE

Out of darkness and peace, Mr. Cecil Barth drifted slowly backward to the consciousness of the glare of the sunshine, of a babel of foreign tongues and of two points of physical anguish, centering respectively in a bruised head and a sprained ankle. He closed his eyes again; but he was unable to close his ears. Still too weak to make any effort upon his own behalf, he wondered vaguely when those clacking tongues would cease, and their owners begin to do something for his relief.

"Stand out of the way, please. He needs air."

The words were English; the accent unmistakably American. Barth pinched his lids together in a sturdy determination not to manifest any interest in his alien champion. For that reason, he missed the imperative gesture which explained the words to the crowd; he missed the anxious, kindly light in Nancy Howard's eyes, as she elbowed her way to his side and bent down over him.

"You are hurt?" she questioned briefly.

Even in this strait, Barth remained true to his training. He opened his eyes for the slightest possible glance at the broad black hat above him. Then he shut them languidly once more.

"Rather!" he answered, with equal brevity.

The corners of Nancy's mouth twitched ominously. It was not thus that her ministrations were wont to be received. Accustomed to fulsome gratitude, the absolute indifference of this stranger both amused and piqued her.

"You are American?" she asked.

This time, Barth's eyes remained open.

"English," he returned laconically.

Again Nancy's lips twitched.

"I beg your pardon. I might have known," she answered, with a feigned contrition whose irony escaped her companion. "But you speak French?"

"Not this kind. I shall have to leave it to you." In spite of the racking pain in his ankle, Barth was gaining energy to rebel at his short sight and the loss of his glasses. It would have been interesting to get a good look into the face of this intrepid young woman who had come to his rescue.

She received his last statement a little blankly.

"But I don't speak any French of any kind," she confessed.

"How unusual!" Barth murmured, with vague courtesy.

Nancy rose from her knees and dusted off her skirt.

"I don't see why. I've never been abroad, and we don't habitually speak French at home," she answered a little resentfully.

Barth made no reply. All the energy he could spare from bearing the pain of his ankle was devoted to the study of how he could get himself out of his present position. His gravelly resting-place was uncomfortable, and it appeared to him that his foot was swelling to most unseemly dimensions. Nevertheless, he had no intention of throwing himself upon the mercy of a strange American girl of unknown years and ancestry. Raising himself on his elbow, he addressed the bystanders in the best Parisian French at his command. The bystanders stared back at him uncomprehendingly.

Standing beside him, Nancy saw his dilemma, saw, too, the bluish ring about his lips. Her amused resentment gave place to pity.

"I am afraid you are badly hurt," she said gently.

"Yes."

"Where is it?"

"My ankle."

"Sprained?"

"Broken, I am afraid." Barth's answers still were brief; but now it was the brevity of utter meekness, not of arrogance.

"Oh, I hope not!" she exclaimed. "You can't walk at all?"

Gritting his teeth together, Barth struggled up into a sitting posture.

"I am afraid not. It was foolish to faint; but I hit my head as I went down, and the blow knocked me out."

As he spoke, he bent forward and tried to reach the laces of his shoe. With a swift gesture, Nancy forestalled him and deftly slipped the shoe from the swollen ankle. Her quick eye caught the fact that few of her friends at home could match the quality of the stocking within. Then her glance roved to his necktie, and she smiled approvingly to herself. In her girlish mind, Barth would pass muster.

Nevertheless, there was nothing especially heroic about him, as he sat there on the gravel with his ankle clasped in his hands and the color rising and dying in his cheeks. A man barely above the middle height, spare and sinewy and without an ounce of extra flesh, Cecil Barth was in no way remarkable. His features were good, his hair was tawny yellow, and his near-sighted eyes were clear and blue.

"Where can I find a surgeon?" he asked, after a little pause.

"I don't know, unless—" Nancy hesitated; then she added directly, "My father is a doctor."

He nodded.

"And speaks English?" he queried.

Nancy bravely suppressed her laughter.

"New York English," she replied gravely.

And Barth answered with perfect good faith,—

"That will do. They are not so very different, and we can understand each other quite well, I dare say. Where is he?"

The girl pointed towards the crest of the bluff.

"He is at the Gagnier farm."

"May I trouble you to send some one for him?" Barth asked courteously.

She glanced about her at the group of French faces, and she shook her head.

"I never can make them understand," she objected. "I'd better go, myself."

But, in his turn, Barth offered an objection.

"Oh, don't go and leave me," he urged a little piteously. "I might go off again, you know."

"But you just said you couldn't walk?" Nancy responded, in some surprise, for, granted that the stranger was able to remove himself, she could see no reason whatsoever that he should not feel free to do so.

"Oh, no. I can't walk a step. My foot is broken," he answered rather testily, as a fresh twinge ran through his ankle.

"Then how can you go off, I'd like to know."

Barth stared at her uncomprehendingly for a moment. Then a light broke in upon his brain.

"Oh, I see. You don't understand. I meant that I might faint away," he explained.

Nancy's reply struck him as being a trifle unsympathetic.

"Well, what if you did?" she demanded. "I can't be in two places at once, and these people won't eat you up. Make up your mind that you won't faint, and then you probably won't."

Barth peered up at her uneasily.

"Are you—are you a Christian Scientist?" he asked.

Nancy's laugh rang out gayly.

"Didn't I say my father was a doctor?" she reminded him. "Now please do lie still and save your strength, and I'll see what I can do about it all."

She was gone from his side only for a moment. Then she came flying back, flushed and eager.

"Such luck!" she said. "Right at the foot of the hill, I found Père Gagnier and the cabbage cart, just coming home from market. He will be here in a minute, and he talks French. Some of these people will carry you to the cart, and you can be driven right up to the door. That will take so much less time than the sending for my father; and, besides, even if he came down, you couldn't be left lying here on the gravel walk for an indefinite period. You would be arrested for blocking the path of the pilgrims, to say nothing of having relays of cripples crutching themselves along over you."

In her relief at having solved the situation, she paid no heed to the stream of nonsense coming from her lips. Barth's stare recalled her to self-consciousness.

"No, really," he answered stiffly.

"Well, daddy?"

At the question, Dr. Howard looked up. Still a little breathless and dishevelled by her hurried scramble up the hill, Nancy stood before him, anxiety in her eyes and a laugh on her lips.

"How is the British Lion?"

"Most uncommonly disagreeable," the doctor answered, with unwonted energy.

"So I found out; but he has occasional lucid intervals. How is his ankle?"

"Bad. For his own sake, I wish he had broken it outright. Nancy, what am I going to do with the fellow?"

Nancy dropped down into a chair, and smoothed her ruffled hair into some semblance of order.

"Cure him," she answered nonchalantly.

The doctor shrugged his shoulders.

"It takes two to make a cure."

"Then hire Père Gagnier to cart him back to Sainte Anne again, and let her try her finger upon him."

In spite of himself, the doctor laughed. Then he grew grave again.

"It's not altogether funny, Nancy. You have unloaded a white elephant on my hands, and I can't see what to do with it."

"How do you mean?" she questioned, for she was quick to read the anxiety in her father's tone.

"The man speaks no French that these people here can understand, and he is going to be helpless for a few days. How is he going to have proper care?"

"Send him in to Quebec. There must be a hospital there."

"I won't take the risk of moving him; not for ten days, at least."

"Hm!" Nancy's falling inflection was thoughtful. "And you came here to get away from all professional worry. Daddy, it's a shame! I ought never to have had him brought here."

Pausing in his tramp up and down the room, Dr. Howard rested his hand on the pile of auburn hair.

"It was all you could do, Nancy. One must take responsibilities as they come."

Nancy broke the pause that followed. Rising, she pinned on her hat.

"Where are you going?"

"To the station. I'll telegraph to Quebec for a nurse. We can have one out here by night. Good by, daddy; and don't let the Lion eat you up."

More than an hour later, she came toiling up the hill and dropped wearily down on the steps.

"No use, daddy! I have exhausted every chance, and there's not a nurse to be had. Quebec appears to be in the throes of an epidemic. However, I have made up my mind what to do next."

"What now?"

"I shall turn nurse."

"Nancy, you can't!"

"I must. You're not strong enough, and such a curiosity as this man mustn't be left to die alone. Besides, it will be fun, and Mother Gagnier will help me."

"But you don't know anything about nursing."

"I won't kill him. You can coach me behind the scenes, and I shall scramble through, some way or other. Besides, the Good Sainte Anne will help me. I've just been tipping her, for the way she has come to my relief. Only this morning, I promised her half a dollar, if she would deign to give me a little excitement." Then the girl turned still more directly to her father, and looked up at him with wayward, mocking, tender eyes. "Daddy dear, this isn't the only emergency we have met, side by side. Mother Gagnier shall do all the rougher part; the rest you shall leave to me. Truly, have you ever known me to fail you at the wrong time?"

And the doctor answered, with perfect truthfulness,—

"No, Nancy; I never have."

CHAPTER FOUR

Out on the end of the long pier that juts far into the Saint Lawrence, Nancy Howard was idly tossing scraps of paper into the choppy surface of the mighty river. Behind her, Sainte Anne-de-Beaupré was rapidly putting on her winter guise. The last pilgrimage ended, the good saint lost no time in packing up her relics for safe keeping, until the next year's pilgrims should turn their faces towards her shrine. Nancy had returned from the telegraph office, two days before, past rows of dismantled booths and of shops whose proprietors were already taking inventory of their remaining possessions. The heaped-up missals and rosaries made little impression upon her; but even her stalwart Protestantism rebelled at sight of the bare-armed priestess who was scrubbing a plaster Virgin with suds and a nailbrush. Nancy would have preferred the more impersonal cleansing administered by the garden hose.

Even Nancy Howard had been forced to admit that the Good Sainte Anne had earned her money. Excitement had not been lacking, during the past two days. It was one thing to come to her father's aid with an offer to play nurse; it was quite another matter to give several hours of each day to the whims of a man who was as unused to pain as he was to the thwarting of his plans. Nancy had expected a playful bit of masquerade. She promptly discovered that she was doomed to work as she had never worked before. She had informed Barth that it was her custom to leave all financial arrangements in the hands of the doctor. She had no idea what value it might have pleased her father to set upon her services. She had a very distinct idea, however, that, whatever the value, she fully earned it. Arrogant and desponding, masterful and peevish by turns, Cecil Barth was no easy patient. Accustomed all his life to being served, he now had less notion than ever of lifting a finger to serve himself. Moreover, Nancy Howard had a rooted objection to being smoked at. Her objection was based upon chivalry, not antipathy to nicotine; nevertheless, it was active and permanent. She only regained her lost poise, when she tried to reduce to systematic orthography the unspellable accent of her patient, most of all that prolonged *Oh-er, raahther!* which appeared to represent his superlative degree of comparison.

"Oh, nurse?"

Barth's voice met her on the threshold, as, capped with a bit of lawn and covered with an ample apron from the wardrobe of Madame Gagnier, she opened the door of the invalid's room.

"Yes, sir."

"I thought you would never come back."

"You have needed something?"

"Yes. The room is too warm, and I think it is time for the rubbing."

"Not for fifteen minutes," Nancy answered calmly. "I told you I would be back in time."

"Yes. But it is so warm here."

"Why didn't you call Madame Gagnier to open a window?"

"Because she is so very clumsy. Please open it now."

Nancy repressed a sudden longing to cross the room on her heels. Barth was sitting up, that day; but the lines around his lips and the brilliant patch of scarlet on either cheek betrayed the fact that the past two days had worn upon him.

"Is your foot aching now?" she asked, as she returned to her seat.

"Yes, intensely. Do you suppose that doctor knows how to treat it?"

Nancy's eyes flashed.

"He ought to," she answered shortly.

Barth turned argumentative.

"It is not a question of obligation; it is a mere matter of training and experience," he observed.

"He is the best doctor in the city," Nancy persisted.

"In Quebec?"

"No; at home."

For the dozenth time since his catastrophe, Barth regretted the loss of his glasses. Nancy's tone betrayed her irritation. Unable to see her face distinctly, he was also unable to fathom the cause of her displeasure. He peered at her dubiously for a moment; then he dropped back in his chair.

"Very likely," he agreed languidly. "Now will you please move the foot-rest a very little to the right?"

"So?"

"Yes. Thank you, nurse."

"Is there anything else?"

He pointed to the table at his elbow.

"My pipe, please; and then if you wouldn't mind reading aloud for a time."

Nancy did mind acutely; but she took up the book with an outward showing of indifference, while Barth composed himself to smoke and doze at his pleasure.

For a long hour, Nancy read on and on. Now and then she glanced out at the sunshiny lawn beneath the window; now and then she looked up at her patient, wondering if he would never bid her cease. In spite of her rebellion at her captivity, however, she was forced to admit that Barth had his redeeming traits. His faults were of race and training; his virtues were his own and wholly likable. Moreover, in all essential points, he was a gentleman to the very core of his soul and the marrow of his bones.

"'Still of more moment than all these cures, are the graces which God has given, and continues to give every day, through the intercession of good Sainte Anne, to many a sinner for conversion to better life.'" Nancy's quiet contralto voice died away, and M. Morel's old story dropped from her hands. Barth's eyes were closed, and she decided that he had dropped to sleep; but his voice showed her mistake.

"It's a queer old story. Do you believe it all, nurse?"

A sudden spice of mischief came into Nancy's tone.

"Yes, and no. I doubt the epilepsy and paralysis; it remains to be seen about the conversions to a better life."

"I suppose one could tell by following up the cases," Barth said thoughtfully.

"Certainly." Nancy's accent was incisive. "I accept nothing on trust."

Barth took a prolonged pull at his pipe.

"But it's not so easy to follow up cases two hundred and fifty years old," he suggested.

Nancy laughed.

"No; I'll content myself with the modern ones."

"Do you suppose there are any modern ones?"

"Oh, yes. The priests claim that there are several new cases, every year."

"And you can get on the track of them?" he asked, with a sudden show of interest.

"Surely. I have my eye on one of them now," Nancy responded gravely.

"A Sainte Anne miracle?"

"Yes."

"Tell me where it is?" he urged.

She shook her head.

"I can't. It concerns somebody besides myself," she replied, with a decision which he felt it would be useless to question.

There was a prolonged pause. It was Barth who broke it.

"Strange we never heard of the place at home!" he said reflectively.

"How long since you came here?" Nancy asked, rather indifferently.

"Two weeks."

"And you like it?"

"For a change. It is a change from the 'Varsity, though."

"Which was your university?" she inquired, less from any interest in the answer than because she could see that her patient was in an autobiographical frame of mind, and even her brief experience of mankind had taught her to let such moods have their way.

"Kings, at Cambridge. I was at Eton before that."

"What sent you out here?"

"Ranching. My brother went in for the army, and we didn't care to have two of a kind in the same family."

"It might be a little monotonous," she assented gravely. "But where is your ranch?"

"I haven't any yet. I am stopping in Quebec for the winter, and I shall go out, early in the spring."

"Is Quebec a pleasant place?" she asked, as she crossed the room to the window and stood looking out at the river beneath.

"It's rather charming, only I don't know anybody there."

"Why don't you get acquainted, then?"

"How can I? I brought some letters; but the people have moved to Vancouver."

"Yes; but they aren't the only people in Quebec."

"Of course not; but I don't know any of the others."

"But you can?"

"How?" Barth queried blankly.

"Why, talk to them, do the things they do—oh, just get acquainted; that's all," the girl answered, with some impatience.

He raised his brows inquiringly. It was not the first time that Nancy had been annoyed by the expression.

"Talk to people, before you have been introduced to them?"

"Yes. Why not?"

"No reason; only it's not our way."

"Whose way?"

"The way we English people do."

"Oh, what a Britisher you are!" she said, with a momentary impatience that led her to forget her self-imposed rôle as hireling.

His lips straightened.

"Certainly. Why not?" he asked quietly.

Baffled, she attempted another line of attack.

"But you were never introduced to me," she told him.

"Oh, no."

"And you talk to me."

"Yes. But that is different."

"How different?" she demanded.

"You are my nurse."

Her color came hotly.

"I wasn't at first."

Too late she repented her rashness, as Mr. Cecil Barth made languid answer,—

"No. Still, if I remember clearly, it was you who first spoke to me. Oh,—nurse!"

But the door banged sharply, and Barth found himself alone with his ankle and with his thoughts.

"Where is the nurse?" he asked Dr. Howard, a long hour later.

"She went out for a walk."

"Again?"

"Yes. Have you needed her?"

"Not exactly; but—" Barth hesitated. Then, like the honest Englishman he was, he went straight to the point. "The fact is, doctor, I am afraid I said something that vexed her. I didn't mean to; I really had no idea of annoying her. I should dislike to hurt her feelings, for she has been very good to me."

For the first time in their acquaintance, Dr. Howard could confess to a liking for his patient. Nevertheless, he only nodded curtly, as he said,—

"You couldn't have had a better or more loyal nurse."

According to her custom, Nancy remained on duty, that evening, until nine o'clock. Then she moved softly up and down, setting the room in order for the night. Barth had been lying quiet, staring idly up at the mammoth shadow of Madame Gagnier, rocking to and fro just outside the door. Then, as Nancy paused beside him, he turned to face her.

"Can I do anything more, sir?" she asked, with the gentle seriousness which marked her moods now and then.

"Nothing, thank you. I am quite comfortable."

"I am glad. I hope you may have a quiet night."

"Thank you. I hope I may. You have been very good to me, nurse, and—" his speech hurried itself a little; "I appreciate it. As I understand, your wa— salary is paid through the doctor; but perhaps some little thing that—"

His gesture was too swift and sure to be avoided. The next instant, Nancy Howard found herself stalking out of the room with blazing cheeks and with a shining golden guinea clasped in the hot palm of her left hand.

CHAPTER FIVE

At her window looking out upon the Ring in the ancient Place d'Armes and upon the Chateau beyond, Nancy Howard stood idly drumming on the pane. Under its gray October sky, the gray-walled city of Quebec had appeared most alluring to her, that morning; but she had turned her back upon its invitation and had resolutely busied herself in settling her own possessions and those of her father in the rooms which had been waiting for them at The Maple Leaf.

Nancy had left Sainte Anne-de-Beaupré with scant regret, the night before. She had spent numberless interesting hours in the society of Mr. Cecil Barth. He had piqued her, antagonized her and occasionally had even compelled her to like him in spite of herself. However, the whole episode had been forced upon her. Now that it was ended, she was glad to dismiss it entirely into the past, and she had not thought it necessary to inform Barth that she too expected to pass some weeks in Quebec. There was scant chance of their meeting again, and Nancy had imagined that she had parted from him without regret.

On his side, Barth had been at no pains to conceal his regrets. As Dr. Howard had reminded him, Nancy had been a most loyal nurse; and the young Englishman took it quite as a matter of course that his attendant should be a girl of brains and breeding as well. He had heard much of the American college girl, and he promptly pigeonholed Nancy with others of that class, although in fact she had been educated by her father and polished by a year or so spent at a famous old school on the Hudson. Barth admired Nancy's brains, her common sense and her alert deftness. To his mind, these qualities in part atoned for her independence and her hot-headed Americanism; but only in part. Her society was often restful, but never cloying; and Barth, now able to hobble about his room, peered mournfully out of his window after his departing nurse with feelings akin to those of a youngster suddenly deprived of his best mechanical toy. Bereft of his nurse, he took to his pipe, smoked himself into lethargy, and emerged from his lethargy so cross that Madame Gagnier, lumbering into the room to settle him for the night, fled from his presence with her cap awry and her checked pinafore pressed to her aged eyes.

Dusk had fallen, when Nancy and her father drove up the steep slope of Palace Hill, passed the Basilica and stopped at the low yellow door of The Maple Leaf. Of the city Nancy saw but little. Of The Maple Leaf, glaring with electric lights, she saw much and, even at the first glance, she assured herself that that much was wholly to her liking. It was not alone the curved ceiling of the entrance hallway, nor the cheery little dining-room where the four tables and the huge mahogany sideboard struggled not to elbow each other in their close quarters; nor yet the deep window-seats of the rooms with their French casements and their panelled shutters. It was the nameless flavor of the place, pervading all things and beautifying all things, the flavor of nothing in the world but of old Quebec. The Chateau might exist anywhere; The Maple Leaf could have existed nowhere outside of the ancient city wall.

"Don't you love it, daddy?" Nancy urged for the third time, as they came up from their late supper.

"It seems very central," the doctor assented tranquilly. "Of course, it is a great advantage for me to be so near Laval. I only hope you won't be lonely here, Nancy."

She laughed scornfully.

"Lonely! After Sainte Anne-de-Beaupré!" she protested.

"The town is often a good deal more lonely than the country," he assured her.

But Nancy, whose eyes had not been entirely busy with the furniture of the dining-room, shook her head. Then she went into her own room, to fall asleep and, quite as a matter of course, to dream that Mr. Cecil Barth, Union Jack in hand, was chasing her around and around the little fountain she could hear plashing down in the Ring.

All the next morning, Nancy was busy in their two adjoining rooms, hanging up her gowns and trying to devise an arrangement which should keep her father's shirts from too close connection with his bottle of ink. Now and then she halted beside his windows which looked down on a gray-walled courtyard where an aged habitant sat on a chopping-block and peeled potatoes without end. Occasionally she wandered back to her own room, and stood gazing out at the Champlain statue by the northern end of the terrace and at the pointed copper roofs of the huge Chateau. Then she went on brushing her father's clothes, and sorting out her own tangle of gloves and belts and the kindred trifles that add a touch of chaos to even the most orderly of trunks. At last, her work done, she smoothed her hair, tweaked her gown into position and, without a glance into the long mirror of her wardrobe, she ran down to the dining-room in search of her father.

She found him the sole occupant of a table near the door, and the other tables were absolutely deserted. As she went back to her room, Nancy was forced to admit that the meal had been a bit dull. A father and daughter who have been constant companions for years, are unable to produce an unfailing stream of brilliant table talk; and Dr. Howard, tired with the effort of getting his bearings in a strange library, was even more taciturn than was his wont.

Accordingly, it was in a mood dangerously akin to homesickness that Nancy left the empty dining-room and returned to her equally empty bedroom. Once inside the door, she made the mortifying discovery that her lashes were wet; and, with a swift realization of the ignominy of her mood, she caught up her hat and coat, and started out to explore the city on her own account.

As she dressed herself for supper, two nights later, Nancy confessed to herself that the past two days were the dreariest days she had ever spent. Totally engrossed in his historical research, her father spent his daytime hours in poring over the manuscripts in Laval library, his evening in rearranging and copying his hurried notes. Left entirely to herself, Nancy discovered the truth of his words, that a town could be far more lonely than the country. At Sainte Anne-de-Beaupré, every one had had a word of greeting for the bright-faced American girl; here it seemed to her that she had no more personality than one of the pawns on a chessboard. She walked the streets by the hour at a time, straying at random from church to church, loitering on the terrace, or tramping swiftly out the Grand Allée far past the Franciscan convent and the tollgate beyond. The tourist season was almost ended. A few honeymoon couples were still straying blissfully about the ramparts; but, for the most part, Quebec had come back from summer quarters on lake and river, and was settling into winter routine. Nancy watched it all with wide, interested, dissatisfied eyes. The show delighted her; but, as at all other shows, she felt the need of some companion whose elbow she could joggle in moments of extreme excitement.

As a part of the show, The Maple Leaf had gratified her whole artistic sense. Humanly speaking, she had found it a bit disappointing. Manœuvre as she would, she could never succeed in finding the dining-room full. There seemed to be something utterly inconsequent in the way in which the boarders took their meals, now late, now early, and now apparently not at all. She had been told that there were forty of them; but, so far as she could discover, six constituted a quorum, and the meal was served accordingly. Once only, the entire quorum had occurred at her own table. Four fresh-faced elderly Frenchmen had marched into the room in procession, and had planted themselves opposite Nancy and her father. Dr. Howard read French, but spoke it not at all. Nancy felt that her own three words would prove inadequate. Accordingly, after one international deadlock over the possession of the salt, silence had fallen. When she left the table, Nancy felt that she had gained a full perception of the viewpoint of a deaf mute.

It was with a spirit of absolute desperation that Nancy flung open the door of her wardrobe, that night. Humanity failing, she would take refuge in clothes. At Sainte Anne, she had lived chiefly in a short skirt and blouse; at The Maple Leaf, she had been waiting to discover the prevailing habits of dress. Now she told herself that two women at a time could not make a habit;

and, furthermore, she assured herself that she cared nothing for local habits anyway. The wardrobe held three new gowns, obviously of New York manufacture. Nancy did not hesitate. With unerring instinct, she chose the most ornate one of the three, which also chanced to be the one which was most becoming.

And so it came to pass that Reginald Brock, pausing in the hall to take off his overcoat, whistled softly to himself as he caught a glimpse of a pale gown of dusky blue and a head capped with heavy coils of tawny hair. The coat slid off in a hurry, Brock gave one hurried look into the tiny mirror of the rack; then, his honest Canadian face beaming with content, he came striding into the dining-room and dropped into his place at Nancy's side, with a friendly nod of greeting.

CHAPTER SIX

Half an hour later, Brock followed Nancy into the parlor. The Lady of The Maple Leaf was at his side, and Nancy had an instinctive feeling that they were in search of her. It was the Lady who spoke.

"Mr. Brock has just been talking to your father in the hall," she said; "and now he has asked me to give him a ceremonious introduction to you. As a rule, we aren't so ceremonious, here in Canada; but Mr. Brock insists upon it that the butter-knife and the mustard are no proper basis for acquaintance."

"I have learned a thing or two from Johnny Bull," the tall Canadian added, as he placed himself in the window-seat beside Nancy's chair.

"Johnny Bull?"

"Yes, an English fellow that has been stopping here for a few days. Where is he? I haven't seen him for a week," he added, turning to the Lady.

"He is ill; I expect him back in a day or two. Please excuse me. I hear the telephone." And she hurried out of the room.

Nancy looked after her regretfully. Even during the three days she had been there, she had gained a sound liking for the blithe little woman, always busy, never hurried, and invariably at leisure for a friendly word with any or all of her great family of boarders. Brock's glance followed that of Nancy.

"Yes, she is a remarkable woman," he assented gravely to her unspoken words. For an instant, his keen gray eyes met Nancy's eyes, steadily, yet with no look of boldness. Then his tone changed. "But about Johnny Bull. He is a revelation to the house, the son of a stiff-backed generation. He was here for a week, and left us all trying to get his accent and to imitate his manners."

"And what became of him?"

"Gone. The Lady says he is ill. I hope we didn't make him so. Have you been here long, Miss Howard?"

"Three days."

"And have you seen anything at all of Quebec?"

"Yes, a little. I have been to the Cathedral, and the Basilica, and the Gray Nunnery, and the Ursuline Convent, and—"

"You appear to be of an ecclesiastical turn of mind," Brock suggested, laughing.

"So does Quebec," she retorted.

He laughed again.

"Yes, I suppose it does to a stranger; but wait till you have been here a little longer."

"What then?"

"You'll forget that a church exists, except the one you go to, on Sundays."

She laughed in her turn.

"Not unless I grow deaf. The Ursuline bell begins to ring at four, and the one on the Basilica at half-past. From that time on until midnight, the bells never stop for one single instant. Under such circumstances, how can one forget that a church exists?"

He modified his statement.

"I mean that you'll find that Quebec has its worldly side."

"Which side?" she queried. "As far as I can discover, the city is bounded on the north by the Gray Nuns, and on the south by the Franciscan sisters. Moreover, I met Friar Tuck in the flesh, down in Saint Sauveur, yesterday."

Brock raised his brows questioningly.

"Do you mean that your explorations have even extended into Saint Sauveur?"

"Yes. Still, there is hope for me. I haven't been to the Citadel yet, and I keep my guide-book strictly out of sight."

"Out of mind, too, I hope," he advised her. "It holds one error to every two facts, and the average tourist carries away the impression that Montgomery was shot in mid-air, like a hawk above a hen-roost. If you don't believe me, go and listen to their comments upon his tablet."

"Where is it?"

"Two thirds of the way up Cape Diamond, above Little Champlain Street. It is labelled as being the spot where Montgomery fell; but, as it is two hundred feet above the road, one can only infer that he came down from somewhere aloft. Is this your first visit to Quebec, Miss Howard?"

"Yes. I have been in Sainte Anne-de-Beaupré for three weeks, though."

"Any pilgrimages?" Brock inquired, as he deliberately settled himself in a less tentative position and crossed his legs. A closer inspection of Nancy was undermining his vigorous objection to red hair, and he suddenly determined that the parlor was a much more attractive spot than he had been wont to suppose.

"One; but it was a large one."

"Miracles, too?"

Nancy laughed.

"One and a half," she responded unexpectedly.

"Meaning?" Brock questioned.

"The half miracle was a man who threw away his crutches and crawled off without them."

"And the whole one?"

Nancy laughed again. Then she said demurely,—

"That the Good Sainte Anne answered my prayer for a little excitement."

"Was that a miracle?"

She answered question with question.

"Did you ever stop at Sainte Anne?"

"Yes, once for the space of two hours. We had all the excitement I cared for, though."

Nancy sat up alertly.

"Was it a pilgrimage?"

"No; merely a pig on the track."

She nestled back again in the depths of her chair.

"What anticlimax!" she protested.

"But you haven't told me what form your own excitement took," Brock reminded her.

"It was an Englishman."

"Oh, we're used to those things," he answered.

"Then I pity you," she said, with an explosiveness of which she was swift to repent. "Oh, I beg your pardon," she added contritely. "Perhaps you are one of them, yourself."

"No; merely a Canadian," Brock reassured her.

"Isn't it the same thing?"

A mocking light came into Brock's gray eyes.

"Not always," he replied quietly.

"No." Nancy's tone was thoughtful. "I am beginning to find it out. Our Englishman was unique."

"Ours?"

"Yes, by adoption. The Good Sainte Anne and I took him in charge."

"With what success?"

"It remains to be seen. We did our best for him; but really he was very preposterous."

"What became of him?"

"Nothing."

"Nothing?"

"No. He is there now; at least, he was there, when we came away."

"Was he working out his novena?"

"No; just mending himself. He fell off from something, his dignity most likely, and bumped his head and sprained his ankle. I happened to be on the spot, and rashly admitted that my father was a doctor. Then, before I really had grasped the situation, the poor man was bundled into a cart and deposited at our door, half fainting and wholly out of temper."

"And then?"

"And then we couldn't get a nurse for love or money, and I had to go to work and take care of him."

"Happy man!" Brock observed. "I only hope he appreciated his luck."

The corners of Nancy's mouth curved upwards, and a malicious light came into her eyes.

"I think he did. He not only expressed himself as pleased with my services; but, on one occasion, he gave me a—"

"A what?"

"A brand-new guinea." And Nancy's laugh rang out so infectiously that Brock would have joined in it, if she had been discussing the foibles of himself rather than of the unknown Englishman.

"How exactly like our Johnny Bull!" he commented, when he found his voice once more.

Suddenly Nancy's puritan conscience asserted itself.

"Truly, I ought not to laugh about him, Mr. Brock. He had no idea that I was anything but a servant, and he thought he had every reason to tip me. He wasn't bad, only very funny. He really knew a great deal and, according to his notions, he was a most perfect gentleman. It was only that our notions clashed sometimes. Yes, daddy, I am coming. Good night, Mr. Brock." And she left him staring rather wishfully after the disappearing train of her dull blue gown.

It must be confessed that Brock dawdled over his breakfast, the next morning; but his dawdling was quite in vain. Nancy had taken her own breakfast long before he appeared, and, by the time Brock had reached his second cup of coffee, she was walking rapidly along the terrace towards the Citadel. At the end, she paused for a moment of indecision. Then, with a glance up at the Union Jack above her head, she slowly mounted the long flight of steps and came out on the narrow upper terrace which skirts the outer wall of the fortress. There she paused again and stood, her arms folded on the railing, looking down on the picture at her feet. She had been there once before; to-day, however, the impression was keener, more enjoyable. The change might have come from the sunshine that lay in yellow splashes over the city beneath; it might have come in part from the memory of her idle talk with Brock, the night before. In all that town of antiquity and of strangers, it had been good to meet some one whose age and viewpoint corresponded to her own. The direct gaze of Brock's clear eyes had pleased Nancy. She had liked his voice, and the unconscious ease with which he carried his seventy-three inches of height. Too outward seeming, his type was as unfamiliar as that of the Englishman, and Nancy liked it vastly better. With Barth, she had been standing on tiptoe, psychologically speaking. With Brock, she could be her every-day, normal self.

It had been at Brock's suggestion that she had gone to the upper terrace, that morning; and she shook off the memory of his gray eyes in order to recall the dozen sentences with which he had characterized the salient points of the view beneath. Then she gave up the attempt. In the face of all that beauty, it was impossible to fix one's mind upon mere questions of geography. At her left, the city sloped down to Saint Roch and the Charles River beyond, and beyond that again was the long white village of Beauport straggling along the bluff above the river. At her right, quarter of a mile beyond the Citadel, were the ruined hillocks of the old French fortifications; and, on the opposite shore, the town of Lévis was crested with its trio of forts and dotted with tapering spires of gray. From one of the piers below, a little steamer was swinging out into midstream and heading towards the point where Sillery church overlooks the valley; and, close against the base of the cliff, the irregular roofs of Champlain Street lay huddled in a long line of shadow. The river was shadowy, too; but above the city a rift in the clouds sent the strong sun pouring down over the guns on the eastern ramparts, over the southern tower of the Basilica and over the spires of Laval. As she looked, Nancy drew a long breath of sheer delight and, all at once and for no assignable cause, she decided that she was glad she had come. Then abruptly she turned her back upon a tall figure crossing Dufferin Terrace, and walked swiftly away past Cape Diamond and came out on the Cove Fields beyond.

When she came in to dinner, she was flushed and animated. As Brock had predicted, she had discovered that Quebec's interest did not centre wholly in its churches. True, there had been a certain disillusion in finding a portly Englishman playing golf with himself upon the ground over which the French troops had marched out to face the invading, conquering foe, in seeing a Martello Tower begirt with clothes-lines and flapping garments, and in discovering a brand-new rifle factory risen up, Phœnix-like, from the ashes of the old-time battleground. The impression was blurred a little; nevertheless, it was there, and Nancy, as her feet wandered up and down the trail of the armies upon that thirteenth of September of the brave year 'Fifty-nine, took a curious satisfaction in the fact that Wolfe, too, had been banned with a head of red hair. Her own ancestors were English. Perhaps some of their kin had landed at Sillery Cove, to scale the cliff and die like gentlemen upon the Plains of Abraham. Her blood flowed more quickly at the thought. In Nancy's mind, this was the hour of England. She even forgot the shining golden guinea that reposed among her extra hairpins.

Nancy came into the house to find the Lady packing a dinner into an elaborate system of pails and cosies. The Lady looked up with a smile.

"Our invalid has come back again," she explained; "and I am sending his dinner over to his room."

CHAPTER SEVEN

"Well," Brock inquired, three days later; "have you been doing ecclesiastics again, to-day?"

Nancy, glancing up from her soup, registered the impression that Brock supported an extremely good tailor, and that his Sabbath raiment was becoming to him.

"Yes. You told me that this was the proper day for it."

"Where did you go?"

"To the Basilica, of course."

Brock smiled.

"True to the tradition of the tourist. By the way, that's rather a good alliteration. I think I'll use it again sometime."

Nancy disregarded his rhetorical outburst and pinned her attention to the fact.

"Do they always go there?"

"Yes, to start with. Of course, you didn't stop there."

"But I did. Why not?"

"Miss Howard, you have neglected your opportunities. The regular tourist itinerary begins with the Basilica at ten, sneaks out and goes over to the English Cathedral at eleven and follows on the tail of the band when it escorts the soldiers home to the Citadel. Then it takes in the Ursuline Chapel at two, stops to drop a tear over Montcalm's skull and then skurries off, on the chance of getting in an extra service before five-o'clock Benedictions at the Franciscan Convent."

"The white chapel with the pale green pillars?"

"Yes, out on the Grand Allée."

"I've been there," she assented. "I love the place."

"And then," Brock continued inexorably; "if you make good time over your supper, you can just get back to the Basilica at seven."

Nancy drew a long breath.

"But I don't need to do all that," she objected. "There are more Sundays coming."

"That makes no difference. Every stranger is bound to gallop through his first Sunday in Quebec. It is one of the duties of the place. You think you won't do it; but, at two o'clock, you'll have an uneasy consciousness that those cloistered nuns over at the Ursuline may do something or other worth seeing. By quarter past two, you'll be buried in a haze of mediævalism and incense."

"Never!" she protested, with what proved to be strict adherence to truth.

"And what about the Basilica?" Brock asked her.

"Superb!" Nancy's eyes lighted. "I was there, a few days ago. It was empty, and it didn't impress me in the least. It seemed to me a dead weight of white enamel paint and gold leaf, so heavy that it wasn't even cheerful. But to-day—"

"To-day?" he echoed interrogatively.

But Nancy made an unexpected digression.

"Mr. Brock, what is that huge pinky-purple Tam O'Shanter dangling above the chancel?"

"Miss Howard, where was your bump of reverence, and where were your guide-books?"

"My bump of reverence was fastened down with hatpins, and my guide-books are buried in the bottom of my trunk."

"Since when?"

"Since I made the discovery that Quebec must be inhaled, not analyzed," she responded promptly.

Brock laid down his knife and fork, and patted his hands together in mock applause.

"A subtle distinction. Might I ask whether it applies to the incense?"

Nancy made a wry face.

"No. Incense should be a symbol, not a fact. It is destructive to all my devotional spirit. Still, even in this one week, I have become an epicure in it. Granted that the wind is in the right direction, I can recognize the brand at least a block away. I like the kind they use at the Basilica best. That out at the Franciscan Convent is doubtless choice; but it is a bit too pungent for my Protestant nose." Then of a sudden her face grew grave. "Please don't think I am making fun of serious matters, Mr. Brock," she added. "Even if I do dislike the incense, I can appreciate the beauty of the service, and I should be ashamed of myself, if I couldn't be really and truly reverent in the midst of all that dignified worship."

Brock was no Catholic; he possessed the average devoutness of his age and epoch. Nevertheless, he liked Nancy's swift change of mood. All in all, he liked Nancy extremely, and he was sincerely grateful to the fate which had given him this attractive table companion. The past three days had brought them into an excellent understanding and friendship. Trained in totally different lines, they yet had many a point in common. They were equally direct, equally frank, equally blest with the saving sense of humor. In spite of the dainty femininity of all her belongings, Nancy met Brock with the unconscious simplicity of a growing boy. The manner was new to Brock, and he found it altogether pleasing. Most of the women he had met, had contrived to impress upon him that he was expected to flirt with them. It was obvious that Nancy Howard wished either to be liked for herself, or to be let alone.

"Then you enjoyed yourself?" he asked.

Nancy's mind went swiftly backward over the morning. Impressionable and artistic of temperament, she could yet feel the thrill which accompanies the worship of close-packed, kneeling humanity, still hear the chanting of the huge antiphonal choirs, the throng of priests in the chancel answered by the green-sashed seminarians in the organ loft above. The gorgeous robes of the celebrants, the ascetic face of the young preacher, and even the motley crowd who, too poor to hire seats in a church of such wealth and fashion, knelt in a huddled mass of humanity upon the bare pavement just within the nave: all these were details; but they helped to fill in a picture of absolute devotion and faith. Nancy raised her eyes to Brock's face.

"I would be willing to pray with a rosary, all my days," she said impulsively; "if it would give me the look of some of those people."

For a moment, Brock felt, the look was hers. Then she laughed again.

"Still, I shall always have one regret. Why didn't you tell me how to make a procession of myself?"

"What do you mean?"

"About the gorgeous man that ushers one in?"

"I didn't know there was one."

"Mr. Brock!"

"Miss Howard?"

"But you ought to."

"But I don't go to the Basilica."

"Not always, of course; but surely sometimes."

"I was never inside the doors."

"I met," Nancy observed reflectively; "a New York man, last summer, who had never set eyes on the Washington Arch."

"Well?"

"Well, the two cases seem to me to be about parallel."

Brock reddened. Nevertheless, it was impossible to take offence at Nancy's downright tone and, the color still in his cheeks, he laughed.

"I may as well plead guilty. But who is the man?"

"The New Yorker?"

"No; the Basilica."

"What is he, you'd better say. He appears to be a mixture of an usher, a tithingman and a glorious personification of the Church Militant. He is at least six feet tall, and he wears a long blue coat with scarlet facings and yards of gold lace. That would be impressive enough; but he gains an added bit of dignity by perambulating himself up the aisles with a tall, gold-headed sceptre in his hand."

"Did he also perambulate you?"

Nancy's head moved to and fro in sorrowful negation.

"No; nobody told me about him, and I lost my chance. I was so disappointed, too. One doesn't get a chance, every day in the week, to be converted into a whole triumphal procession with an ecclesiastical drum-major at its head."

"Most likely it is only a Sunday luxury there," Brock suggested dryly. "But what did you do?"

Nancy's face lengthened.

"I disgraced myself," she confessed. "But how could I know the customs of the country? I went in good season, and I stood back, meekly waiting for an usher, until the whole open space around me was full of men, kneeling on handkerchiefs and newspapers and even on their soft hats. I began to feel like a Tower of Babel set out in the middle of a village of huts. I know I never was half so tall before. And still no usher came. At last, I couldn't bear it any longer, and I sneaked into an empty pew, half-way up the aisle."

Brock nodded.

"Oh; but it wasn't at all the right thing to do. I was barely seated, when I felt a forefinger poke itself into my shoulder. I looked around, and there stood a woman in crape, frowning at me as if I were a naughty child. She whispered something to me. It sounded very stern; but I couldn't understand what it was about, so I just smiled at her and started to move in. But she poked me again, quite viciously, that time, and pointed out into the aisle. Then I understood her."

"And obeyed?" Brock asked, laughing.

"What else could I do? She was taller than I."

"And then?"

"Then the Good Samaritan appeared."

"The gold-laced one?"

"No; nothing so impressive. He was a little Frenchman who came out of his pew farther down the aisle, and in the nicest possible English asked me to go there with him. You've no idea how merciful he was to me, nor how I appreciated it. I was beginning to feel like an outcast, and he saved my self-respect and returned it to me, unbroken."

Brock started to answer; but Dr. Howard had appealed to Nancy for confirmation of one of his statements. By dint of much effort and at cost of frequent misunderstandings, the good doctor had established relations with his neighbor across the table, and the two men had been toiling through a prolonged conversation. Concerning mere matters of theory, each fondly imagined that he understood the other perfectly. Confronted with the problem of the ultimate destination of the sugar-bowl, they lost their bearings completely, and were forced to supplement their tongues with the use of their right forefingers.

Nancy's acquaintance with the row of Frenchmen was limited to the careful distribution, at every meal, of exactly two little nods apiece, one of hail, the other of farewell. Since her first meeting with Brock, she had been surprised at the chance which had continually brought them into the dining-room at the same hour; and, in her absorption in his talk, one or other of the Frenchmen was often half through his deliberate meal before she remembered to deal out to him his nod of greeting. She liked them well enough; but, at the present stage of intercourse, they seemed to her a good deal like well-bred automatons.

While Nancy talked to her father, Brock eyed her furtively. She wore a dark green gown, that noon, and her vivid hair was piled high in an intricate heap of burnished coils. Her hands were bare of rings, her whole costume void of the dangling ornaments which Brock so keenly detested; but, close in the hollow of her throat, there blazed one great opal like a drop of liquid fire.

So suddenly that he had no time to drop his eyes to his plate, Nancy turned to him.

"Mr. Brock, there is my French Samaritan!" she exclaimed softly.

Brock glanced up at the figure who was moving past the table where they sat.

"That? That is St. Jacques," he said.

"Who is he?"

"A law student, over at Laval, and one of the best fellows walking the earth at the present time," Brock answered, with the swift enthusiasm which, as Nancy discovered in the weeks to come, was one of his most striking characteristics.

Nancy rested her elbows on the table, with a fine disregard of appearances.

"Well, he looks it," she said impressively.

"He's all right." Brock nodded over his grapes.

"And lives here?"

"Eats here; that's all. The table just back of you is full of Laval men. They come in relays, twenty of them for the six seats; and Johnny Bull sits enthroned among them like a mute at the funeral feast. St. Jacques sits just back of your father. I wonder you haven't noticed him before."

Nancy played aimlessly with her grapes for a minute or two. Then, turning slightly in her chair, she looked over her shoulder towards the next table. As she did so, the man who sat exactly at her back, moved by some sudden impulse, turned at the same instant, and Nancy found herself staring directly into the unrecognizing eyeglasses of no less a person than Mr. Cecil Barth.

CHAPTER EIGHT

To adopt the vernacular of the stables, Nancy shied violently, for the apparition was both unexpected and unwelcome. She rallied swiftly, however, and, promptly resolving to make the best of a bad matter, she gave a little nod and smile of recognition. The next instant, both nod and smile went sliding away from the unresponsive countenance of Mr. Cecil Barth and focussed themselves with an added touch of cordiality upon M. St. Jacques, while the young Frenchman bowed low in surprised pleasure at her friendly greeting.

Even in her instantaneous glance, Nancy saw that Barth looked worn and ill; and, with unregenerate spite working in her heart, she told herself that she was glad of it. She had no idea that, unable to supply himself with new glasses before his return to the city, Barth had gained absolutely no conception of the personal appearance of his quondam nurse. Moreover, as Nancy had neglected to inform him in regard to her normal pursuits and her future plans, he had spent the last week in regretfully picturing her, still in cap and pinafore, ministering to the needs of some invalid Yankee in that vast unknown which he vaguely termed The States. Accordingly, it came about that the dinner, that Sunday noon, was finished in hot rage by Nancy, in joyous anticipation by Adolphe St. Jacques, and in stolid unconcern by Mr. Cecil Barth who was aware neither of the existence of an emotional crisis, nor of the fact that to him was due any share of its creation.

Nancy sat alone in the parlor, after dinner, waiting for her father to join her, when Barth came into the room. He halted on the threshold long enough to look her over in detail; then he limped past her and took possession of the chair beyond her own. As they sat there silent, elbow to elbow, Nancy was conscious of a wayward longing to remind him that it was high time for his liniment. However, she refrained. Two could play at that game of stolid disregard.

The Lady looked puzzled, as she followed Barth into the room, a few moments later. Only a day or two before, Nancy, moved by a spirit of iniquity, had confided to the Lady the whole tale of her connection with Barth, and the Lady, who already adored Nancy and, moreover, was discerning enough to see the inherent manliness of Barth, had held her peace. A charming scene of recognition was bound to follow Barth's return to The Maple Leaf. No hint of mystery to come should take from the glamor of that pleasant surprise. Barth and Nancy both were curiously alone; both were aliens, meeting upon neutral soil. Already in her mind's eye the Lady foresaw romance and international complications.

With her bodily eye the Lady saw the elements of her international complications sitting in close juxtaposition, but with their backs discreetly turned to an obtuse angle with each other. She made a swift, but futile, effort to account for the situation. Then she gave Nancy a merry nod of comprehension, if not of understanding, and passed on to speak to Barth.

"You are better, to-day, I hope."

"Oh, yes."

"I hope you didn't feel obliged to come over to dinner. It was no trouble to send your meals to you."

"Oh, no. I was tired of stopping in my room."

"You look as if you had been having rather a hard time of it," the Lady said kindly.

"Yes. I never supposed an ankle could be so painful. Still, I hope it is over now."

"Then it doesn't trouble you to walk?"

"Oh, rather! And, besides, it makes one such an object, you know, and then people stare. It won't be long, though, I dare say, before I can walk without limping."

A naughty impulse seized upon the Lady.

"You were at Sainte Anne-de-Beaupré, you said? And could you get proper care in so small a place?"

Over the unconscious head of Mr. Cecil Barth, Nancy shook her fist at the Lady. Then she fled from the room; but not quickly enough to lose Barth's answer,—

"Oh, so-so; nothing extra, but still quite tolerable. The doctor was clever; but the nurse, his daughter, was an American, a good-hearted sort of girl, but rather rude and untrained."

All that Sunday afternoon, Nancy cherished her hopes of vengeance. Plan after plan suggested itself to her fertile brain, was weighed and found wanting. Planned hostility was totally inadequate; she would leave everything to chance. Nevertheless, Nancy tarried long at her mirror, that night; and she went down to supper with her head held high and a brilliant spot of color in either cheek. As she passed the parlor door, she saw Barth, book in hand, seated exactly where she had left him, and she suddenly realized that, rather than endure the short walk to his room, he had chosen to spend his afternoon in the dreary solitude of a public sitting-room. For an instant, her heart smote her, and her step lagged a little; then she remembered the guinea, and recalled Barth's words, that noon, and her step quickened once more.

Brock followed her back to the parlor.

"Oh, let the Basilica go, to-night," he urged.

"But you told me it was a part of my itinerary."

"No matter. You haven't kept up your round, to-day, anyway. Did you do the Ursulines, this afternoon?"

"No. I was all ready to go; but something happened that put me in an unchurchly frame of mind," Nancy said vindictively.

"Just as well. It makes people suspicious of your past habits, if you rush too violently into church-going."

"But twice isn't too violently."

"Two is too," he retorted. "Besides, St. Jacques asked me to ask you if he might be formally introduced, to-night."

Nancy's face brightened, and her voice lost the little sharp edge it had taken on with her reference to her encounter with Barth.

"Of course. Both on account of his courtesy to me, and of your characterization of him, I shall be delighted to meet him. Where is he?"

Over in his corner by the window, Barth glanced up from his book. Voices rarely made any impression upon him; but something in Nancy's tone caught his fancy, reminded him, too, of an indefinite something in his past. With calm deliberation, he fumbled about for the string of his glasses, put them on and favored Nancy with a second scrutiny, critical and prolonged. The girl's cheeks reddened under his gaze, and instinctively she turned to Brock for protection; but Brock had gone in search of his friend. From across the room, one rose from a group of women and came to Nancy's rescue.

"Mr. Barth?" she said interrogatively, in her pretty broken French. "I think it is Mr. Cecil Barth; is it not? My friend, Mrs. Vivian, has written to me about you. I believe you brought a letter, introducing yourself to her."

Instantly, though a little stiffly, Barth rose to his feet. This acquaintance, at least, could show its proper credentials.

"And have you met Miss Howard?" she continued, after a moment's talk. "Miss Howard, like yourself, is a stranger among us. Perhaps she will allow me to introduce Mr. Cecil Barth."

"Howard appears to be rather a common name, here in Canada," Barth observed.

"Really? I've not met any one else by the name," Nancy answered rashly.

"Yes. It was the name of my nurse."

"Your—nurse?"

"Yes. I don't mean the nurse who took care of me when I was a little chap," Barth explained elaborately. "I've just been ill, you know, sprained my ankle out here at Sainte Anne-de-Beaupré and was laid up for two weeks. My nurse out there was a Miss Howard, Miss Nancy Howard; but she was an American."

Something in the cadence of the final word was displeasing to Nancy, and the edge came back into her voice.

"What a coincidence!" she observed quietly. "I am an American, myself, Mr. Barth."

Barth's answer was refreshingly naïve.

"Oh, really? But nobody would ever think it, I am sure."

It was two days before Nancy met Barth again. From her window, she watched with pitiless eyes as he hobbled to and from his meals, and her strategic position enabled her to avoid the dining-room while he was in it. Meanwhile, her acquaintance with the Lady and St. Jacques had made rapid strides and, together with Brock, omnipresent and always jovial, they formed a merry group in the tiny office where the Lady mothered them all by turns. Nancy shunned the parlor in these latter days. Dr. Howard was increasingly absorbed in his studies; and Nancy felt the increasing need of a duenna, as it dawned upon her more and more clearly that, wherever she went, there Brock and St. Jacques were sure to follow. Nancy looked at life simply; these healthy-minded boys were only a pair of excellent playmates. Nevertheless, all things considered, Nancy preferred to play in the society of an older person. Furthermore, for long hours at a time, Mr. Cecil Barth sat enthroned in the parlor; and, by this time, Nancy was resolved to avoid Mr. Cecil Barth at any cost.

The gray October noon was cool and sweet, two days later, when Nancy came tramping down the Grand Allée. The exhilaration of a long walk was upon her, and her step was as energetic as when she had left The Maple Leaf, early that morning. Starting at random by way of the Chien d'Or and the ramparts, she had skirted the Upper Town and come out by Saint John's Gate to the Saint Foye Road which she had followed until the monument *Aux Braves* was left far behind and the glimpses of the dark blue Laurentides were lost in the nearer trees. Then, turning sharply to the eastward, she came into the Grand Allée not far from the shady entrance to Mount Hermon. A glance at her watch assured her that the morning was nearly over, and she sped along the interminable plank sidewalk at a pace which should bring her back to the tollgate in time for the short detour to the Wolfe monument. Once in sight of that inscription, grand in its simple brevity, Nancy invariably forgot the present, forgot the gray wall of the jail close by, forgot even the insistent voices that hailed her from the cab-stand at the gate. For the moment, she stood alone in the presence of the past and of that daring leader whose destiny forbade his entering the stronghold he had conquered.

Her breath coming quickly and her lower lip caught between her teeth, Nancy stood leaning against the rail, looking out across the Plains. So absorbed was she in her day-dream of the past that she paid no heed to a cab which halted at her side.

"Oh, Miss Howard?"

Starting abruptly, she turned to face Barth. Tired of his solitary drive, the young fellow's eyes were smiling down into the familiar face as, hat in hand, he bent forward in eager greeting.

Nancy's day-dream vanished like a broken Prince Rupert's drop.

"Good morning, Mr. Barth," she said grimly.

"It is a jolly sort of morning; isn't it? You are paying homage to my countryman?" he inquired.

The allusion was unfortunate. It recalled his last words to Nancy, and she grew yet more grim.

"Brave gentlemen belong to no country," she answered, with what seemed to her a swift burst of eloquence.

Barth laughed.

"Poor beggars! Must they all be expatriated? If that's the case, it's better to be whimpering over a sprained ankle than to die victorious on the Plains of Abraham."

"That wasn't what I meant at all," Nancy interposed hastily. Then she took out her watch and looked at it a little ostentatiously. "It is a glorious day, Mr. Barth, and I wish you a pleasant drive. It is nearly dinner time, and I must hurry on."

"Why not let me take you in?" he urged. "I am going directly back to The Maple Leaf."

But Nancy's answer permitted no argument.

"Thank you, no. I am out for the exercise, and you are going on farther. It is impossible for me to interfere with your drive." And, with a curt bow, she turned away and stalked off in the direction of the Grand Allée.

The light died out of Barth's eyes and the friendly smile fled from his lips, as he realized that, for the first time in his life, he had had his overtures rejected. Worst of all, the rejection was by an American and, from his point of view, totally without cause. Mr. Cecil Barth dropped back in his seat, stretched out his lame foot into a position of comparative comfort, and then said Things to himself.

He passed Nancy just outside the Saint Louis Gate. Head up, shoulders thrown back, she was swinging along with the free step of perfect health and equally perfect content. From the solitary dignity of his cab, Barth eyed her askance.

"Wait a bit, though," he apostrophized her, with a sudden burst of prophecy. "The time will come, Miss Howard, when you don't rush off and leave me alone like this."

But Nancy, rosy and flushed with exercise, entered the dining-room, that noon, without a glance in his direction. Barth kept his own eyes glued to his plate; but, from over his right shoulder, he could hear every word of her merry talk with Reginald Brock. As he listened, Barth began to question whether England might not have allowed too great a share of independence to certain of her western colonies.

CHAPTER NINE

"Miss Howard?"

Nancy glanced up, as St. Jacques appeared in the doorway with Brock at his side. At the farther end of the room, Barth also glanced up. The action was wholly involuntary, however, and Barth sought to disguise with a yawn his ill-timed manifestation of interest.

"You look as if you had something of importance to announce," Nancy replied, as she rose and crossed the room to the door.

"So we have. What are you going to do, this evening?"

"That isn't an announcement; it is a question," she suggested.

St. Jacques laughed. Nancy always enjoyed the sudden lighting of his face. At rest, it was almost heavy in its dark, intent earnestness; at a chance word, it could turn mirthful as the face of a child, gentle with the sympathetic gentleness of a strong man. Just now, the rollicking child was uppermost.

"How can I tell the difference? I am not English," he answered.

Nancy cocked the white of one eye towards the far corner of the room.

"Neither am I," she said demurely.

Brock's answer was enigmatic; but Nancy held the key.

"It is always possible to be grateful to Allah," he said, low, but not so low as to keep the color from rising in Barth's cheeks.

St. Jacques turned suddenly.

"Good evening, Mr. Barth. Is your ankle better?" he queried.

But Barth was as yet unable to make any distinctions in measuring out his displeasure.

"Thank you, Mr. St. Jacques," he answered icily. "It is almost quite well."

"O—oh. I am very glad," St. Jacques responded, in such vague uncertainty as to how great a degree of gain might be represented by the *almost quite* that he entirely missed the note of hostility in Barth's voice.

Again the white of Nancy's eye moved towards the corner of the room, as Brock said,—

"But you haven't answered St. Jacques's question, Miss Howard."

"I beg your pardon. I am not going to do anything, unless sitting in this room counts for something."

"But it doesn't." Barth took an unexpected plunge into the conversation.

"Then what makes you do it?" Brock inquired.

His intention had been altogether hostile, for he had been irritated by the discourtesy shown to his friend. Nevertheless, his irritation gave place to good-tempered pity, as the young Englishman answered quietly,—

"Because there's not so very much left that I can do. One doesn't get much variety in a radius of half a mile a day."

This time, Nancy turned around.

"Doesn't that ligament grow strong yet?" she asked, in a wave of sympathy which swept her off her guard.

Then she blushed scarlet, for Barth was looking up at her in manifest astonishment. How could this impetuous young woman have discovered the fact that he owned a ligament? He had not considered it a fit subject for conversation. Was there no limit to the unexpected workings of the American mind?

"I didn't know—Oh, it is better," he answered.

Then in a flash the situation dawned upon Brock. He recalled Barth's unexplained illness; he remembered Nancy's story of the Englishman and his golden guinea. Back in the depths of his sinful brain he stored the episode, ready to be brought out for use, whenever the time should be ripe. And Nancy, looking into those clear gray eyes, knew that he knew; knew, too, that it would be useless to beg for mercy for the unsuspecting Britisher. Moreover, she was not altogether sure that she wished to beg for mercy.

"But really, have you any plan for this evening?" St. Jacques was urging.

Dismissing the others from her mind, Nancy smiled into the dark face which was almost on a level with her own.

"Nothing at all."

"That is good. There is a little opera at the Auditorium, to-night; nothing great, but rather pretty. I saw it in Saint John, last year. Brock and I both thought—"

"What time is it now?" Nancy asked.

"About seven."

Nancy reflected swiftly. Then she said,—

"Impromptu parties are always the best. Go and ask the Lady if she can come with us. If she will—"

But only Barth in his corner heard the ending of her sentence.

Half an hour later, Nancy came rustling softly down the stairway, her shining hair framed in the white fur ruff of her cloak. Two immaculate youths were pacing the hall; but Barth had disappeared. She found him sitting in the office beside the Lady. He rose, as Nancy appeared in the doorway.

"Don't let me keep you," he said regretfully. "You are going out?"

In his present mood of content, St. Jacques felt that he could afford to be gracious.

"Don't we look it?" he asked boyishly.

Experience had taught Nancy what to expect when Barth fell to fumbling about the front of his waistcoat. Nevertheless, even she blushed at the prolonged stare which was too full of interest to be impertinent. Then, without a glance at the others, Barth let the glasses fall back again.

"Oh, rather!" he answered, with unwonted fervor.

The Lady laughed.

"Is that the best you can say of us, Mr. Barth?" she inquired.

"*Rather* is Barth's strongest superlative," Brock commented. "Well, are we ready?"

The Lady rose with some reluctance. During the few days of his imprisonment, she had been brought into closer contact with Barth. She had watched him keenly, and she had come to the conclusion that, underneath all his haughty indifference, the young Englishman was lonely, homesick and altogether likable.

"It is really too bad to turn you out, Mr. Barth," she said kindly. "Won't you stay here and read? It is more cosy here, and you can be quite by yourself."

The friendly words touched Barth and, for an instant, he lost his poise. A sudden note of dejection crept into his voice, as he answered,—

"I seem to accomplish that end, wherever I go."

Brock was already leading the way to the door, and Nancy was gathering up her long skirt. It was St. Jacques who lingered.

"Perhaps you would like to go with us," he suggested.

"Oh, I—" Barth was beginning, when the Frenchman interrupted,—

"We shall be very glad to have you, and I can easily telephone for another seat. It is not a great opera; but it will be better than sitting alone in your room."

The unexpected addition to their party was by no means to Nancy's liking. Nevertheless, her eyes rested upon St. Jacques with full approval. The deed had been a gracious one, and Nancy felt that, with Brock and St. Jacques to help her, she could easily manœuvre Barth to the outer seat beyond the Lady.

The event justified her belief. Barth demurred, then yielded to a second invitation which was cordially echoed by the Lady; and it was at the Lady's side that he limped down the aisle. Nancy, in the rear with the others, told herself that he had no need for his profuse apologies regarding his dress. Even in morning clothes, Barth showed that both his figure and his tailor were irreproachable. She also told herself that, until then, she had had no notion of the way the man must have suffered. It is not without reason that a man of the early twenties allows himself to hobble ungracefully into a strange theatre, or gets white at the lips, by the time he is finally seated.

As St. Jacques had said, the opera was by no means a great one. However, Nancy, sitting in that dull green interior, looking about her at the half-veiled lights and at the dainty gowns, was absolutely content. Barth, at the farther end of the row, was talking dutifully to the Lady, and Nancy had no idea that his position, bending forward with his hands clasped over his knee, was taken for the sole purpose of being able to watch herself. Brock was for the moment wholly absorbed in a scrutiny of the audience, and Nancy settled back at her ease and fell into idle talk with St. Jacques.

Already the young Frenchman was assuming a prominent place in her thoughts. He was serious without being dull, merry without being frivolous; and Nancy rarely found it needful to explain to him the unexpected workings of her somewhat inconsequent mind. Even Brock was sometimes left gasping in the rear. St. Jacques, although by different and far less devious paths, was generally waiting to meet her, when she reached her new viewpoint.

Little by little, she had come to know much of his history. The strong habitant blood of two hundred years before had brought forth a line of sturdy, earnest professional men. True to their ancestry, they had made no effort to shake off its customs or its tongue. Highly educated, first at Laval, then at Paris, they had gone back to the simple life of their own people, to give to them the fruits of what, generations before, had been taken from them. Because the primeval St. Jacques had wrested supremacy from his neighbors, there was no reason that his son's sons should turn their backs upon their less fortunate brothers, and seek wealth and fame in the luxury-loving cities to the southward. St. Jacques was of the physical type of the old-time habitant; but developed far towards the level of all that is best in manhood. The defensive instincts of a young girl are not always unreliable. Nancy trusted Adolphe St. Jacques implicitly. She was sure that he never stopped to question how to show himself loyal and courteous; it came to him quite as a matter of course.

"But you speak English at home?" she asked him.

"No; only French."

"Then you surely have been trained in an English school," she persisted.

He shook his head.

"The school was like Laval, all French."

"And yet, you speak as we do."

His lower lip rolled out into his odd little smile.

"As you do, but more slowly. Of course, I understand; but I think in French, and it takes a little time to put it into English. But my English is not like Mr. Barth's."

"Nor mine," she assured him merrily.

But he met her merriment with a curiously grave face.

"Miss Howard, I do not see why I can't like that fellow," he said thoughtfully.

"Nor I. And yet, he isn't half bad," Nancy replied, with unexpected loyalty.

"I know. He is intelligent, and he means to be a gentleman," St. Jacques answered, frowning gravely as he argued out the position. "I think I see his good points; but I have nothing that—that is in common with any of them. Our worlds are different, and we can never bring them into connection."

For the moment, Nancy lost her own gayety and spoke with a seriousness which matched his own.

"I think I understand you. I have felt it, myself. It is not anything he does consciously, yet he leaves me feeling that we have absolutely no common ground. By all rights, we Americans ought to feel kinship with the English; but—"

St. Jacques turned to face her.

"But?" he echoed.

However, Nancy's eyes were fastened on her fan, and she answered, with the fearless honesty of a boy,—

"But now and then I have felt, since I came here, that my likeness was entirely to the French."

And St. Jacques bowed in silence, as the curtain rose for the final act.

Just then, there came an unexpected scene and one not down upon the programme. The soprano was already in place and the tenor, in the wings, was preparing to rush in to kneel at her feet, when the manager came out across the stage. In the midst of the gaudy costumes, his black-clothed figure made an instantaneous impression, an impression which was heightened by his level voice.

"Ladies and gentlemen, I regret to be obliged to announce to you—"

Brock never knew from what corner of the upper gallery came that shrill, insistent cry of fire. When he realized his surroundings, he was bracing himself against the seat in front of him, his whole tall figure tense in the effort to keep Nancy from being crushed by the mad rush for the doors. Then, with a bound, the young Frenchman vaulted over the seat towards the other end of the row.

"Look out for the Lady, Brock," he ordered, as he dashed past. "Some one must help Barth. His foot is giving out, and he will drop, in a minute."

Then, as swiftly as it had arisen, the panic died away. Again and again the orchestra pounded out *God Save the King* with an energetic rhythm which could not fail to be reassuring. The tumult in the galleries subsided; one by one, in shamefaced fashion, the people came straggling back to their seats. Brock was mockingly recounting the list of his bruises, while the manager completed his ill-timed announcement of the sudden illness of one of the singers. Then the curtain was rung down and rung up again for a fresh start. Just as it shivered and began to rise, Barth bent forward.

"Oh, Mr. St. Jacques."

"Yes?"

"I have to thank you for your help. I needed it, and it was given in a most friendly way."

St. Jacques had no idea of what those few words cost the dignity of the taciturn young Englishman. Otherwise, he would have framed his answer in quite another fashion. As it was, he shook his head.

"You count it too highly," he said, with dry courtesy. "In our language we call such things, not friendship, but just mere chivalry."

And Nancy, though unswerving in her loyalty to St. Jacques, felt a sudden pity for Mr. Cecil Barth, as he shut his lips and leaned back again in his chair.

CHAPTER TEN

"Daddy dear?"

Nancy's accent was a little wishful, as she turned her back on the habitant in the courtyard and faced her father by the dressing-table.

"Yes." The doctor was absently rummaging among his neckties.

"Can't you spare time to go out with me, this afternoon?"

"Where?"

"Anywhere. Lorette, or Beaumanoir, or even just up and down the city. You really have seen nothing of Quebec, daddy, and I—once in a while I get lonely."

The doctor dropped his neckties and looked up sharply.

"Lonely, Nancy? I am sorry. Do you want to go home?"

"Oh, no!" The startled emphasis of her accent left no doubt of its truthfulness.

"Then what is it, child?"

"Nothing; only—It is just as I said. Now and then I feel a little lonesome."

The doctor smiled at his own reflection in the mirror.

"I thought Brock and the Frenchman looked out for that, Nancy."

"They do," she returned desperately; "and that is just what worries me. It makes me feel as if I needed to have some family back of me."

Gravely and steadily the doctor looked down into her troubled eyes.

"Has anything—?"

Nancy raised her head haughtily, as she answered him.

"No, daddy; trust me for that. The boys are gentlemen, and, besides, they treat me as if I were a mere cousin, or something else quite unromantic. I like them, and I like to talk with them. It is only—"

Her father understood her.

"I think you do not need to be anxious, Nancy. Over the top of my manuscripts, I keep a sharp eye out for my girl. And, besides, it is a rare advantage for you to have the friendship of the Lady. Even if I were not here, I would trust you implicitly to her care."

Nancy nodded in slow approval.

"Yes, and she is one of us. Sometimes I am half jealous of her. M. St. Jacques is her devoted slave."

"What about Brock?"

Nancy laughed with a carelessness which was not entirely feigned.

"Mr. Brock burns incense before every woman, young or old. He is adorable to us all, and we all adore him. Still, he never really takes us in earnest, you know."

"I'm not so sure of that," the doctor said, with sudden decision.

"You like Mr. Brock?" she questioned.

"Yes. Don't you?"

"I should be an ungrateful wretch, if I didn't." Then she added, "Speaking of ungrateful wretches, daddy, was anything ever more strange than the whole Barth episode?"

"Haven't you told him yet?"

"Told him! How could I? It is all I can do not to betray myself by accident; I would die rather than tell him deliberately. But I can't see how the man can help knowing."

"Extreme egotism coupled with extreme myopia," the doctor suggested.

"Exactly. If it were one of us alone, I shouldn't think so much about it; but it is a mystery to me how he can see us both, without having the truth dawn upon him."

The doctor pondered for a moment.

"Do you know, Nancy, I believe I haven't once come into contact with the fellow. Except for the dining-room, I've not even been into the same room with him. It is really wonderful how little one can see of one's neighbors."

Nancy faced back to the window with a jerk.

"And also how much," she added mutinously.

But the doctor pursued his own train of thought.

"After all, Nancy, it may be our place to make the first advances. We are older—at least, I am—and there are two of us. He may be waiting for us to recognize him. I believe I'll look him up, this evening, and tell him how we happen to be here."

Nancy faced out again with a second jerk.

"Daddy, if you dare to do such a thing!"

"Why not? After all, I rather liked Barth."

"I didn't."

"But surely you thought he was a gentleman," the doctor urged.

"After a fashion," Nancy admitted guardedly. "Still, now that I have met him, I'd rather let bygones be bygones. It would be maddening, for instance, just when I was sailing past him on my way in to supper, to have him remember how I used to coil strips of red flannel around his aristocratic ankle. No; we'll let the dead past bury its bandages and water them with its liniment, daddy. If I am ever to know Mr. Cecil Barth now, it must be as a new acquaintance from London, not as my old patient from Sainte Anne-de-Beaupré."

"And yet," the doctor still spoke meditatively; "Barth appreciated you, Nancy, and he was certainly grateful."

The girl laughed wilfully.

"He appreciated his hired nurse, daddy, and he was grateful to me to the extent of paying me my wages. By the way, I'd like that money."

"For what?"

"I would drop it into the lap of the Good Sainte Anne. It is no small miracle to have delivered a British Lion into the hands of an American and allowed her to minister to his wounded paw. It was a great experience, daddy, and, now I think of it, I would like to reward the saint according to her merits."

The doctor's eyes brightened, as he looked at her merry face.

"Wait," he advised her. "Even now, the miracle may not be complete."

She ran after him and caught him by the lapels of his collar.

"Oh, don't talk in riddles," she protested. "And, anyway, promise me you won't tell any tales to Mr. Barth."

"My dear child, I have something to do, besides forcing my acquaintance upon stray young Englishmen who don't care for it."

She kissed him impetuously.

"Spoken like your daughter's own father!" she said approvingly. "Now, if you really won't go out to play with me, I'm going to the library to read the new magazines."

An hour later, Nancy was sitting by a window, *Harper's* in her lap and her eyes fixed on the dark blue Laurentides to the northward. The girl spent many a leisure hour in the grim old building, once a prison, but now the home of a little library whose walls breathed a mingled atmosphere of mustiness and learning. Ancient folios were not lacking; but Kipling was on the upper shelves and one of the tables was littered with rows of the latest magazines.

To-day, however, Nancy's mind was not upon her story, nor yet upon the Laurentides beneath her thoughtful gaze. The episode of the previous night had left a strong impression upon her. It was the first time she had seen the three men together; she had watched them with shrewd, impartial eyes. Britisher, Canadian, and Frenchman, Catholic and Protestant: three more distinct types could scarcely have been gathered into the narrow limits of an impromptu theatre party. Beyond the simple attributes of manliness and breeding, they possessed scarcely a trait in common. In two of them, Nancy saw little to deplore; in all three, she saw a good deal to like.

Barth she dismissed with a brief shake of her head. He was undeniably plucky, far more plucky than at first she had supposed. To her energetic, healthy mind, there had been nothing so very bad about a sprained ankle. A little pain, a short captivity, and that was the end of it. Once or twice it had seemed to her that Barth had been needlessly depressed by the situation, needlessly unresponsive to her efforts to arouse him. It was only during the past few days that she had seen what it really meant: the physical pain and weariness to be borne as best it might, in a strange city and cut off from any friendly companionship. It even occurred dimly to her mind that Barth was not wholly responsible for his chilly inability to make new friends, that it was just possible he regretted the fact as keenly as any one else. Moreover, Nancy was just. She admitted, as she looked back over those ten days at Sainte Anne-de-Beaupré, that Barth had been singularly free from fault-finding and complaint. She also admitted that his ignoring of their past relations was no mere matter of social snobbery. Mr. Cecil Barth was totally ignorant of the identity of his former nurse. Having exonerated him from the charge of certain sins, Nancy dismissed him with a shake of her head.

Upon Brock and St. Jacques, her mind rested longer. Until the night before, they had seemed to her to be a pair of boon comrades. While their holiday lasted, they would make merry together. When she turned her face to the southward, the bonds of their acquaintance would drop apart, and their lives would spin on in their individual orbits. Now, all at once, she questioned. The naked impulses of humanity show themselves in times of danger. At last night's alarm, both Brock and St. Jacques had turned instinctively to her protection. Then the difference had showed itself. Brock had given his whole care and strength to her alone. St. Jacques had swiftly assured himself that she was in safe hands; then, with a caution to Brock to guard the Lady, he had thrown himself to the rescue of Mr. Cecil Barth, not because he liked Barth, but because his instincts were all for the succoring of the weak. All night long, Nancy had gloried in Brock's strength and in the singleness of his devotion. Nevertheless, she was woman enough to glory still more in the more prosaic gallantry of the dark-browed little Frenchman. As a rule, the pretty girl in evening dress is prone to inspire more chivalry than a taciturn Britisher of chilly manners and unflattering tongue.

Suddenly Nancy buried her nose in her story. Barth had come into the library and seated himself at the table close at her elbow. When she looked up again, he had put on his glasses and was waiting to meet her eye. She nodded to him, and, before she could go back to her magazine again, he had turned his chair until it faced her own. Over the blue Laurentides the twilight was dropping fast. Upstairs in the dim gallery the librarian was moving slowly here and there among his books. Otherwise the place was quite deserted, save for the two young people sitting in the sunset glow.

"And is this one of your haunts, too, Miss Howard?" Barth asked, as he tossed his magazine back to the table.

The matter-of-course friendliness of his tone struck a new note in their acquaintance. Nancy liked it.

"Yes, I often come here, when it is too stormy for walking," she assented.

"You walk a great deal?"

"Endlessly. Still, it doesn't take so many steps to circumnavigate this little city, I find. I love to explore the out-of-the-way nooks and corners; don't you?"

"I did, until I was cut off in my prime. I had only had two weeks, before disaster overtook me."

This time, Nancy was mindful of her incognito.

"You broke your ankle, I think?" she said interrogatively.

"Sprained it. It amounts to the same thing in the end."

"Was it long ago?"

"Three weeks. Sometimes three weeks become infinite."

"Was it so painful?"

"Yes, especially to my pride. It's so babyish to be ill."

"But you weren't babyish at all," Nancy protested courteously.

Barth stared blankly at her for a minute. Then he laughed.

"You flatter me. Still, it's not well to take too much on trust, Miss Howard. But I am glad if I've gained any reputation for pluck."

Nancy interposed hastily.

"How did it happen?"

"I don't know. The last I remember beforehand, I was standing on the steps of Sainte Anne, watching a pilgrimage getting itself blessed. The next I knew, I was lying on my back on the ground, with my ankle twisted into a knot, and my future nurse taking full possession of my case. That was your namesake, Miss Howard."

"Indeed. Was—was she—pretty?" Nancy inquired, not quite certain what she was expected to say next.

"I never knew. My glasses were lost in the scrimmage, and I can't see ten inches from my nose without them. I couldn't very well ask her to come forward and be inspected at any such range as that. I was sorry, too. The girl really took very good care of me, and I grew quite fond of her. Behind her back, I used to call her my Good Sainte Anne. She was Nancy, you know."

Nancy's magazine slid to the floor.

"Did she know it?" she asked, smiling a little at her awkward efforts to reach the book.

"Allow me," Barth said gravely. "No; I am not sure that she did."

"When you meet her, next time, you can tell her," Nancy advised him.

Barth shook his head.

"I am afraid I never shall meet her."

"The world is very tiny," Nancy observed sententiously. "As a rule, the same person is bound to cross one's trail twice."

"And, besides, even if I did meet her, how could I ever know her?"

"How could you help it?" she queried, smiling into his face which seemed to her, that afternoon, to be curiously boyish and likable.

"But I have no idea how she looked."

"You would know her voice."

"Oh, no. I notice voices; but I rarely remember them."

"But her name?"

"It is of no use, just Nancy Howard. Such a commonplace sort of name as that is no clue. Why, you may be a Nancy Howard, yourself, for anything I know to the contrary."

Nancy laughed, as she rose.

"I might also be your nurse," she suggested. "Stranger things than that have happened, even in my experience, Mr. Barth. However, when you do meet your Nancy Howard, I hope you will tell her that you liked her."

The young fellow looked up at her a little eagerly.

"Do you suppose she would mind about it?"

"Women are generally glad to know when they are liked," Nancy said sagely.

"But most likely she knew it, without my telling."

Nancy shook her head.

"More likely she never guessed it. You probably lorded it over her and treated her like a servant."

To her surprise, Barth blushed scarlet. Then he answered frankly,—

"How you do get at things, Miss Howard! The fact is, I tipped the girl, one night. It seemed to me then merely the usual thing to do. Since then, I haven't been so sure. She was quite a lady, and—"

Nancy interrupted him ruthlessly.

"How did she take it?" she demanded.

"As she would have taken a blow on the cheek. I meant it well. I had given her a bad day of it, and I thought it was only decent to make up for it. I wish now I hadn't; but I couldn't well ask for the money again, though I knew from the way her heels hit the floor that she was wishing she could throw it back at me. Do you know," Mr. Cecil Barth added thoughtfully; "that I sometimes think our English ways aren't always understood over here."

And, in that instant, Nancy forgave the existence of the golden guinea, still reposing among her superfluous hairpins.

"Not always," she assented. "Still, if you were to tell your Nancy Howard what you have just told me, I think she would understand."

"Oh, but I couldn't do that," Barth protested.

"I don't see why not. Very likely she is no more formidable than I am. Anyway, I advise you to try."

As she stood smiling down at him, there came a click, and the dusky library was flooded with the blaze from a dozen electric bulbs. They both winced at the unexpected glare; then Nancy's eyes and Barth's glasses met in a steady gaze. His face was earnest; hers merry and altogether winsome. Suddenly she held out her hand.

"Good by, Mr. Barth," she said kindly. "I am glad you have told me about this."

He rose to his feet.

"You are going? May I walk back with you?"

"Thank you so much for offering. It would be a pleasure; but Mr. Brock is waiting outside to take me for a turn on the terrace."

And, the next instant, Barth was left alone with the librarian.

CHAPTER ELEVEN

"Prove it," Nancy said defensively.

"I will."

"Now."

"Give me time."

"Time is something one seizes, not takes as a free gift."

Brock laughed.

"Your utterances make superb epigrams, Miss Howard. The only objection to them arises when one stops to find out what they really mean."

"I mean that you can never prove to me that the French are really outclassed by the English," she retorted, bringing the discussion back to its point of departure.

Brock looked down at her quizzically.

"Shall St. Jacques and I fight it out in three rounds?" he inquired.

"That's no test. You're not English."

"Not in the real sense of it. But neither is he French. We're both of us relative terms."

"And so useless for the sake of argument," she replied.

"For the sake of nothing else, I trust," Brock said lightly.

She looked up at him with a smile.

"Mr. Brock, I am not an ingrate. Without you and M. St. Jacques, I should have been a good deal more lonely, this past month. My father is an old man, and not strong. He has appreciated your courtesy to him, too."

Brock shifted his stick to his left hand.

"Shall we shake hands on it?" he said jovially. "The month has been rather jolly for us, as Barth would say. The Maple Leaf is a mighty good sort of place; but the atmosphere there is sometimes a little more mature than one cares for. St. Jacques and I haven't given all the good times. But about the argument: when can you take time to be convinced?"

"By a walk to the Wolfe monument?" she queried mockingly.

"No; by two hours of eloquent pleading on my part. I propose to do it by sheer weight of intellect and statistics. How about to-morrow afternoon at three?"

"Very well," she assented.

"I'll cut the office for the afternoon. Shall we choose the Saint Foye Road for the scene of the fray?"

"As you like," she answered merrily. "But remember that you are to do no monologues. I reserve the right to interrupt, whenever I choose."

Then they fell silent, as they tramped briskly up and down the terrace. The lights from the Frontenac beside them glowed in the purple dusk and mingled with the glare that lingered in the west. At their feet, the streets of the Lower Town were crowded in the last mad scurry of the dying day, and the river beyond was dotted here and there with the moving lights of an occasional ferry. Then a bugle call rang down from the Citadel, and Nancy roused herself abruptly.

"I suppose we really ought to go to supper," she said regretfully.

"It isn't late."

"No; but my father will be waiting."

Reluctantly Brock faced about.

"Well, I suppose there are more days to come," he observed philosophically.

"Especially to-morrow," she reminded him.

Barth was at the table, when they entered the dining-room. Eager, flushed with her swift exercise in the crisp night air and daintily trim from top to toe, Nancy seemed to him a most attractive picture as she came towards him. Brock was close behind; together, they were laughing over some jest of which he was in ignorance. Nevertheless, Nancy paused beside his chair long enough to give him a friendly word of greeting, and Barth smiled back at her blissfully. For an instant, it occurred to him that it was rather pleasant to be no longer on the outer edge of The Maple Leaf. At a first glance, he had resented the supremacy of this American girl in an English house. The shorter grew his radius, however, the surer grew his allegiance to the focal point. American or no American, Nancy was undeniably pretty, her gowns threw the gowns of his own sisters into disrepute, and, moreover, that afternoon, she had shown herself altogether friendly and womanly and winning. Accordingly, he sowed the seeds of incipient indigestion by bolting his supper at a most unseemly speed, in order to gain possession of a chair near the parlor door. Close study of the situation, during many previous evenings, had informed him that this chair held a position of strategic importance. As a rule, St. Jacques had occupied it, while Barth had rested on his dignity in remote corners. With the tail of his eye, Barth had assured himself that the Frenchman was at the final stage of the meal, when he himself reached the table. However, the Frenchman was munching toast and marmalade in a most leisurely fashion, turning now and then for a word with Brock and Nancy; and Barth felt sure that he could overtake him. His surety increased as St. Jacques, abandoning his toast, took possession of a mammoth bun and a fresh supply of marmalade. Barth, who scorned all things of the jammy persuasion, finished his meat with the greed of a half-grown puppy, scalded his throat with the tea which had obstinately resisted his efforts to cool it, and, with a brief nod to St. Jacques, left the table and betook himself to the parlor.

"Monsieur has a haste upon himself, to-night," St. Jacques observed dryly.

His early training had been potent, and St. Jacques no longer wasted upon Barth any conversational efforts whatsoever. In Nancy's presence, he treated the Englishman with distant courtesy. In the face of Brock's teasing, he gave him an occasional grudging word of moral support; but, at the table, he ignored him completely. According to the creed of Adolphe St. Jacques, a man should never allow himself to be snubbed twice by the same person. He carried his creed so far that, waitresses failing, he chose to rise and march completely around the table rather than ask for a stray pepper-pot lodged at Barth's other hand.

By the time Barth had gone twice through the diminutive evening paper, advertisements and all, he came to the tardy conclusion that the race was not always to the swift. He knew that Brock had left the house. Hat in hand, the tall Canadian had come into the parlor for a book. The next minute, the front door had slammed, and Brock's measured stride had passed the parlor windows. Brock gone, Barth wondered what could be keeping Nancy. Not even a healthy American appetite could linger for an hour and a half over a meal of cold beef and marmalade.

He started upon a third tour of the paper, in true British fashion beginning with the editorials, and finally losing himself in an enthusiastic account of a recent opening of fall hats. By the time he realized that he was mentally trying each of the hats upon Nancy Howard's auburn hair, he also realized that it was time he roused himself to action. Letting the newspaper slide to the floor, he rose and walked out into the hall. From the office beyond, there came the low, continuous buzz of earnest voices. Rising on his toes, Barth peered cautiously around the corner. Then he seized his hat and stick and, stamping out of the house, banged the street door behind him. The Lady was temporarily absent. In her place, the office chair was occupied by Nancy and comfortably settled opposite to Nancy was M. Adolphe St. Jacques.

Laval had a banquet at the St. Louis, that night. It began late and ended early. From certain random words he had overheard, Barth knew that St. Jacques was not only to be present, but was to be one of the speakers. Accordingly, a personal animosity mingled with his annoyance at the sounds from next door which broke in upon his dreams. The singing was off the key; the cheering was harsh and unduly loud, and when at last *God Save the King* was followed by a rush into the quiet street, Barth crawled out of bed and stood shivering at the window, as the tri-colored banner and its accompanying crowd marched past his ducal residence. In his present mood, it would have been a consolation to have seen that St. Jacques was the worse for his revel. However, that consolation was denied him. In the sturdy color-bearer heading the line, he failed to recognize his table companion; the other revellers tramped along as steadily as did the soldiers going home from church parade. In the depths of his swaddling blankets, Barth shivered. He shivered again, as he crawled back into the icy sheets which he had thoughtlessly left open to the chill night air.

His spirits rose, next morning, when he discovered that St. Jacques did not appear at breakfast. They fell again, when Nancy also failed to appear. His masculine mind could not be expected to discern that she had risen early, in order to attack a basket heaped with long arrears of undarned socks and flimsy stockings. His near-sighted eyes had not discovered Nancy, sitting at her own front window, with a stout number thirteen drawn on over her slender hand. Nancy saw him, however; and, in the midst of her musings, she took friendly note of the fact that, this morning, Barth scarcely limped at all.

Barth loitered in his room until the dinner hour was past. To the Lady he gave the excuse of important letters; but a copper coin would have paid the postal bills incurred by his morning's work. The honest fact was that he longed acutely for more of Nancy's society, and he had no idea how to set about obtaining it. To ask it would be too bald a compliment; he lacked the arrogant graces of his Canadian rivals who appropriated the girl promptly and quite as a matter of course. Barth had been used to more deliberate and tentative methods. Nevertheless, as he stared at the yellow walls of his room, he took a sudden resolve. English methods failing, he would, according to the best of his ability, adopt the methods of America. In his turn, he too would take possession of Nancy. With Nancy's possible wishes in the matter, he concerned himself not at all.

"Too bad it rains!" Brock said, as he met Nancy at dinner, that noon.

"Because you must delay your argument?"

"No. Because we can't have it in the open air. The Saint Foye Road must be changed for the parlor."

"Can you do it there?"

"Why not? It is always empty, in the afternoon."

"I didn't mean that. But will there be room for you there?" Nancy questioned, with lazy impertinence. "I have always noticed that a man needs to gesticulate a great deal, whenever he is arguing for a lost cause."

Brock laughed, as he patted his side pocket.

"Don't be too sure it is lost. You haven't seen my documents yet. Can you be ready, directly after dinner?"

"As soon as I see my father off. Else he would be sure to forget his goloshes and neglect to open his umbrella. A father is a great responsibility; isn't it, daddy?" she added, with a little pat on the gray tweed sleeve.

Nearly an hour later, Barth bounced into the room. By largesse wisely distributed, he had gained a good dinner, in spite of his tardiness. He had found Brock's coat hanging on the rack where he had left his own; and experience had taught him where Brock, once inside The Maple Leaf, was generally to be found. The office was quite deserted; and, with unerring instinct, Barth betook himself in the direction of the parlor.

In the angle behind the half-shut door, at a table covered with maps and papers, Brock and Nancy sat side by side. They looked up in surprise, as Barth dashed into the room.

"Good afternoon, Miss Howard," he said abruptly.

It was Brock who answered.

"You appear to be in haste about something," he remarked.

"Oh, no. I have no engagement for the afternoon. I just looked in to see if Miss Howard—"

Again it was Brock who answered.

"Miss Howard has an engagement."

"To—?" Barth queried, as he edged towards Nancy's side of the table.

Craftily Brock avoided the ambiguous preposition.

"Miss Howard and I are busy together, this afternoon."

"Oh, really. I am very sorry. I hope I don't intrude." And, with the hope still dangling from his lips, Barth plumped himself down on the sofa beside them and felt about for his glasses. As soon as they were found and settled on his nose, he turned to Nancy. "I do hope I'm not in the way," he reiterated spasmodically.

Brock was growling defiantly in his throat; but Nancy's answer was dutifully courteous.

"Not at all, Mr. Barth."

"You are sure you wouldn't rather I went away?" he persisted.

"It isn't our parlor," Nancy reminded him.

"Yours by right of possession." As he spoke, Barth arose and carefully closed the door.

"Oh, no. And we could easily move out."

Barth looked startled. It was hard enough to force himself to this cheerful arrogance of manner. It was harder still to have the manner miss fire in this fashion. It was thus, to his mind, that Brock was accustomed to take forcible possession of Nancy's leisure hours. He had never heard her suggest the advisability of moving out, when Brock came in upon the scene. Vaguely conscious that something was amiss, Barth nevertheless persevered in his undertaking.

"Oh, but why should you move out?"

Nancy's eyes lighted, half with amusement, half with impatience. What was the man driving at? Only yesterday she had been ready to accept him as a friend, as a man of tact and ingrained breeding. Now his former obtuseness seemed to have returned upon him, fourfold. And she had just been explaining to Brock that the man wasn't half bad, after all. The question of what Brock must be thinking of her taste lent an added tinge of acidity to her reply.

"Merely in case you wished to move in," she answered, with the lightest possible of laughs.

Barth turned scarlet; but he valiantly sought to explain.

"But I only came in here, because I was looking for you."

From a man of Barth's previous habits of speech, this was rather too direct. In her turn, Nancy became scarlet.

"What did you wish, Mr. Barth?"

"Oh, just to—to talk to you. It is a beastly day, you know; and I thought—I fancied—"

Nancy cut in remorselessly. Instead of recognizing Barth's imitation of the American manner, she came to the swift conclusion that his vagueness was due to temporary dementia.

"I am sorry, Mr. Barth; but I am very busy with Mr. Brock. Don't let us drive you away, though. We can go to the office."

"But don't do that. Stay here. That's what I came for. I fancied you would like to have a little more talk about Sainte Anne."

Nancy felt Brock's keen gray eyes fixed upon her, felt the world of merriment in their depths. She reflected swiftly. During the past twenty hours, there had been scant chance that Barth should have discovered her identity. His suggestion was doubtless only the random result of chance. Nevertheless, with Brock's eyes upon her, she was unable to parry the suggestion with her wonted ease.

"Why should I care to talk about Sainte Anne?" she asked coldly.

"I—I thought you seemed interested, last night."

Again Nancy felt Brock's eyes on her, and she chafed at the false position in which she found herself. It was plain that Brock took it for granted that she had decoyed the unsuspecting Barth into telling over the tale of his experiences; and Nancy, rebelling at the suspicion, was powerless to deny it. She felt a momentary pity for the young Englishman who seemed bent upon offering himself up as a victim to his allied foes, yet she found it impossible to come to his rescue without imperiling her secret.

Suddenly Barth spoke again.

"Were you ever at Sainte Anne-de-Beaupré, Miss Howard?"

There was an instant's pause, when it seemed to Nancy that Brock must be able to count the throbbing of her pulse. Then she answered quietly,—

"Once, quite a long time ago. However, the whole episode is so unpleasant that I rarely allow myself to think much about it. Mr. Brock, perhaps we'd better go out to the office, if Mr. Barth will excuse us."

CHAPTER TWELVE

Nancy spent the evening in the Valley of Humiliation, Barth spent it in the office with the Lady.

"But what did you say to irritate her?" the Lady asked at length, when Barth, by devious courses, had brought the conversation around to Nancy.

"Oh, nothing. I wouldn't irritate Miss Howard for any consideration," he returned eagerly.

"But she was irritated."

"Y—es; but I didn't do it."

The Lady smiled. Liking Barth as she did, she could still realize that his point of view might be antagonistic to a girl like Nancy. Moreover, she too had seen Barth, that noon. She too had wondered at the unaccountable elation of his manner; and she had recorded the impression that, when a narrow Britisher begins to expand his limits, the broad American would better make haste to seek shelter.

"Tell me all about it," she said kindly.

Barth's feigned arrogance of manner had fallen from him; it was a most humble-minded Britisher who stood before the Lady, and the Lady pitied him. Barth's eyes looked tired; the corners of his mouth drooped, and dejection sat heavy upon him.

The Lady turned a chair about until it faced her own.

"Sit down and tell me all about it, Mr. Barth," she repeated.

Barth obeyed. Later, alone in his room, he wondered how it was that he had been betrayed into speaking so frankly to a comparative stranger; yet even then he felt no regrets. A petted younger son, he had been too long deprived of feminine companionship and understanding. Now that it was offered, he accepted it eagerly. Moreover, Barth was by no means the first lonely youth to pour the story of his woes into the Lady's ear.

Seated with the light falling full upon his honest, boyish face, he plunged at once into his confession, with the absolute unreserve that only a man customarily reserved can show.

"It is just a case of Miss Howard," he said bluntly. "She is an American, and not at all like the girls I have known, treats you like a good fellow one minute, and freezes you up the next. I can't seem to understand her at all."

"What makes you try?" the Lady asked.

It never seemed to occur to the young fellow to blush, as he answered,—

"Because I like her a great deal better than any other girl I ever saw."

In spite of herself, the Lady smiled at the unqualified terms of his reply.

"It hasn't taken you long to find it out."

"No. But what's the use of waiting to make up your mind about a thing of that sort?" Barth responded, as he plunged his hands into his trouser pockets. "You like a person, or else you don't. I like Miss Howard; but, by George, I can't understand her in the least!"

"Is there any use of trying?" the Lady inquired.

Barth stared at her blankly.

"Oh, rather! How else would I know how to get on with her?"

"But, by your own story, you don't succeed in getting on with her."

Barth closed the circle of her argument.

"No. Because I can't seem to understand her."

"Are you sure she understands herself?"

"Oh, yes. Miss Howard is very clever, you know."

"Perhaps. It doesn't always follow. And are you sure she cares to have you understand her?"

The young Englishman winced at the question.

"What should she have against me?" he asked directly.

"I am not saying that she has anything," the Lady answered, in swift evasion. "Sometimes it is to their best friends that girls show their most contradictory sides."

"Oh. You mean it is one of her American ways?"

"Yes, if you choose to call it that."

Barth shook his head.

"Miss Howard is very American," he observed a little regretfully.

The Lady smiled.

"And, my dear boy, so are you very British."

"Of course. I mean to be," Barth answered quietly.

"And perhaps Miss Howard finds it hard to understand your British ways."

Barth looked perplexed.

"Oh, no. I think not," he said slowly. "She never acts at all embarrassed, when she is with me. In fact," he laughed deprecatingly; "I am generally the one to be embarrassed, when we are together."

There was a short pause. Then Barth continued thoughtfully, as if from the heart of his reverie,—

"And I didn't like her especially, at first. She seemed a bit—er—cocksure and—er—energetic. Now I am beginning to like her more and more."

"Have you seen much of her?"

Barth shook his head.

"No. It is only once that we have had any real talk together. That was yesterday, at the library. It's a queer old place, and one talks there in spite of one's self. We had a good time. But generally those other fellows are around in the way."

The Lady raised her brows interrogatively.

"Mr. Brock and that Frenchman," Barth explained. "They are always with her; they haven't any hesitation in coming into the drawing-room and carrying her off, just as I am getting ready to talk to her."

A blot on the Lady's account book demanded her full attention for a moment. Then she looked up at Barth again.

"Why don't you try the same tactics?" she asked.

"I beg your pardon?"

"Why don't you carry her off, just as Mr. Brock is getting ready to talk to her?"

"Because he is so quick that he gets right about it, before I have time to begin. Mr. Brock has a good deal of the American way, himself," Mr. Cecil Barth added, with an accent of extreme disfavor.

The Lady smiled again.

"I think you'll have to develop some American ways, yourself, Mr. Barth," she suggested.

Again the note of dejection came into his voice.

"I tried. Tried it, this afternoon."

"And?" she said interrogatively.

"It was all wrong."

"How do you mean?"

"I don't know. I thought I did it just as Mr. Brock does. I went into the drawing-room and found them together, just the way he has so often found us. I began to talk to her just as he does, only of course I wouldn't think of chaffing her. You know he chaffs her, and she can't seem to make him stop," Barth added, in hasty explanation.

"What did you talk to her about?" the Lady queried.

"That's just it. I didn't get started talking at all. I just asked her if she wouldn't like to talk."

Once more the Lady bent over the blot.

"What did you invite her to talk about?" she asked quietly.

"Sainte Anne-de-Beaupré and all that."

There was a pause. Then,—

"Go on," said the Lady.

"We'd been talking about it in the library, just the afternoon before, and she seemed interested, asked about my accident and my nurse and all. Really, we were just beginning to get on capitally, when she had to go. I thought the best thing to do would be to begin where we left off; but she turned very cross, wouldn't say a word to me and finally picked up her books and walked out of the room. I don't see what I could have done to displease her." And, putting on his glasses, Barth stared at the Lady with disconsolate, questioning blue eyes.

The Lady laughed a little. Nevertheless, she felt a deep longing to scold Nancy, to give Fate a sound box on the ear and to take Mr. Cecil Barth into her motherly embrace. She liked his frankness, liked the under note of respect which mingled in his outspoken admiration for Nancy. She could picture the whole scene: Barth's nervous assumption of ease confronted with the nonchalant assurance of Brock, Nancy's hidden amusement at the tentative request for polite conversation, and her open consternation at the subject which Barth had proposed for discussion. It was funny. She looked upon the scene with the eyes of Nancy and Brock, yet her whole womanly sympathy lay with the Englishman, an open-hearted, tongue-tied alien in a land of easy speech. Barth's hand rested on the corner of her desk. Bending forward, she laid her own hand across his fingers.

"Don't worry, Mr. Barth," she said kindly. "You and Miss Howard will be good friends in time. It is an odd position, your meeting here on neutral soil. Your whole ways of life are so different that you find it hard to understand each other. I am half-way between you, and I know you both.

What is more, I like you both, and I'd like to see you good friends. Leave something to time, and a great deal to Miss Howard. And—forgive me, my dear boy, but I am quite old enough to be your mother—I would let the American ways take care of themselves, and just be my own English self. If Miss Howard is going to like you at all, it will be for yourself, not for any misfit manners you may choose to put on."

"But, the question is, is she going to like me at all?" Barth said despondingly.

The Lady's eyes roved over him from the parting of his yellow hair to the toes of his unmistakably British shoes.

"Forgive my bluntness," she said, with a smile; "if I say that I don't see how she can very well help it."

Half an hour later, she knocked at Nancy's door.

"May I come in?" she asked blithely. "All the evening, I have been talking to a most downcast young Englishman, and now I have come up to administer justice to you. The justice will be tempered with mercy; nevertheless, I think you deserve a lecture."

"Your Englishman is an idiot," Nancy observed dispassionately; "and I don't deserve any lecture at all. However, go on."

Crossing the room, the Lady turned on the electric light.

"Nancy Howard," she said sternly; "your voice was suspicious enough; but your eyes betray you. You've been crying."

"What if I have?" the girl asked defiantly.

The Lady's quick eye caught the glitter of a gold coin on the dressing-table. Then she turned back to Nancy.

"Girls like you don't cry for nothing," she remarked. "May I sit down on the bed?"

Nancy nodded. Then she replied to the first remark.

"I wasn't crying for nothing. I was crying over my conscience."

"What has your conscience been doing?"

"Pricking," the girl answered frankly. "I hate to be nasty to people; but now and then I am driven into it."

"Mr. Barth?"

"Yes, Mr. Barth," Nancy assented, with an accent of finality. "Now go on with your lecture."

The Lady laughed.

"Really, Nancy, you sometimes take away even my Canadian breath. I can imagine that you leave Mr. Barth gasping."

"Mr. Barth would gasp in a stilly vacuum," Nancy replied tranquilly.

"Very likely. It is possible that you might do likewise. But to my point. Was it quite fair, Nancy, to encourage the boy to talk about the Sainte Anne-de-Beaupré episode, and then snub him, the next time he alluded to it?"

"Did he tell you any such tale as that?" Nancy demanded, in hot wrath.

"He—he implied it."

"And you believed him?"

"I—I couldn't understand your doing it." The Lady began to wonder whether the promised lecture were to be given or received.

Nancy sprang up and walked the length of the room.

"Oh, the horrid little cad!" she said explosively.

The Lady turned champion of the absent Englishman.

"He's not a cad, Nancy; he is a thoroughbred little Englishman. I have seen his type before, though never so extreme a case. He is frank and honest as a boy can be. He's born to his British ways, as we are born to ours. It is only that you're not used to him, and don't understand him."

"He doesn't leave much to the imagination," Nancy observed scathingly. Then she dropped down beside the Lady, and looked her straight in the eyes. "I don't want you to be thinking horrid things of me," she said slowly. "I don't want you to think I have been two-sided with Mr. Barth. After what happened at Sainte Anne-de-Beaupré, I have tried to keep out of his way as much as possible. It has been a miserable chance that has brought us into such close quarters; a recognition wasn't going to be pleasant for either of us. But, every time I meet the man, he seems possessed with an insane desire to babble to me about his ankle. I could tell more about it than he can, for I was in league with the doctor, and heard all the professional details. A dozen times, I have been on the very verge of betraying myself. Last night, it reached a climax. He found me alone in the library, and he began to talk. Really, he was more agreeable than I ever knew him before. But you know how it is: the presence of a grass widow always moves you to rake up all the divorce scandals of your experience. Before we had talked for ten minutes, the man was calmly informing me that he was really very fond of his nurse, that, in the secret recesses of his heart, he called her his Good Sainte Anne, that he wished he could meet her again, and finally that he was very sorry he had tipped her."

"Indeed!"

"No; I don't mean that," Nancy protested hastily. "You are the disloyal one now. He didn't imply that she had not deserved the tip. His regrets were for sentimental reasons, not frugal. He was very nice and honest about it, and I never liked him half so well."

"And showed it," the Lady added gently.

"Very likely I did. I don't see why not. But, to-day!" Nancy paused.

"What happened?"

"Didn't he tell you?"

"Only his side of it. Still, I could imagine the rest."

"No; you couldn't. No one could, without having seen it. He came dashing, fairly splashing, into the parlor where Mr. Brock and I were squabbling over politics. Only a little while before, I had been defending him to Mr. Brock, telling him that Mr. Barth was really a gentleman and clever, that I liked him extremely. And then, on the heels of that statement, the man came whacking into the room, interrupted our talk without a shadow of an apology and then, after acting like a crazy being, he capped the climax of his sins by specifically inviting me to talk to him some more about Sainte Anne."

"Well?"

"Well."

The rising cadence was met by the falling one. Then silence followed.

"Well," Nancy resumed at length; "you see my predicament. Mr. Brock knows the whole story; I let it out to him, the day we met. I had no idea I should ever meet Mr. Barth again, and I used no names. Mr. Brock patched together the two ends of the story, and told M. St. Jacques; and it has been all I could do to keep them from using it as an instrument of torture on poor Mr. Barth. To-day, I knew Mr. Brock was furious at him; I knew he was longing to say something, and, worst of all, I knew he thought, as you did, that I had been coaxing Mr. Barth to make an idiot of himself."

"Well?" the Lady said again.

"And he does it, without being coaxed," Nancy responded mutinously. Then she relented. "But he was so pitifully bent on making a fool of himself, just when I had been pleading his cause to the very best of my ability! He babbled at us till I was on the very verge of frenzy. Stop him I could not. He absolutely refused to know when he was snubbed. At last, I fled from the scene and took Mr. Brock with me, and, for all I know to the contrary, the man may be sitting there in the parlor, babbling still."

Nancy laughed; but the tears were near the surface.

"And then?" the Lady asked gently.

"Then I came up here and bemoaned my sins," Nancy answered, with utter frankness. "I hate to be hateful; but I lost my head, and couldn't help it. Now I am sorry, for I truly like Mr. Barth, and I know I scratched him till he felt it clear down through his veneering. He has not only spoiled my whole evening; but, worse than that, I have an apology on my hands, and I really don't see how I am going to make it, without being too specific."

CHAPTER THIRTEEN

Thirty-six hours after his banquet, St. Jacques reappeared in the dining-room. Barth eyed him narrowly.

"Back again?" Nancy queried in blithe greeting.

"At last."

"It was a good while. How are you feeling?"

Barth felt a shock of surprise. Did American girls have no reservations?

"A good deal the worse for wear," the Frenchman was replying, with equal frankness.

Nancy laughed.

"Any particular spot?" she inquired.

"Yes, my head. There's nothing much to show; but it feels swollen to twice its usual size, to-day."

"I am so sorry," she answered sympathetically. "Can I do anything for it?"

St. Jacques laughed, as his face lighted with the expression Nancy liked so well.

"Does your pity go a long way?" he asked.

"At your service."

"To the extent of a walk, after dinner?"

"Yes, if you feel up to it," she answered. "It is a delightful day, and you know I want to hear all about it."

Towards the middle of the morning, Barth sought the Lady.

"Really, it is none of my affair; but what is the girl thinking of?" he demanded.

The Lady's mind chanced to be upon the problem involved in a departing waitress.

"What girl?" she asked blankly.

"Miss Howard."

"What is the matter with Miss Howard now?"

"I don't know. What can she be thinking of, to go for a walk with a man in his condition?" he expostulated.

"Whose condition?"

"That French Catholic, Mr. St. Jacques."

"But there's nothing wrong with his condition. It is only his head," the Lady explained.

"Oh, yes. That is what I mean. She knows it, too."

"Of course. We all know it, and we all are so sorry."

Barth was still possessed of his self-made idea, and continued his argument upon that basis.

"Naturally. One is always sorry for such things. Sometimes even good fellows get caught. Still, that is no reason a girl should speak of it, to say nothing of going to walk with the fellow. Really, Miss Howard's father ought to put a stop to it."

This time, even the Lady lost her patience.

"Really, Mr. Barth, I don't see why. On your own showing, you asked Miss Howard to let you walk home from the library with her, two days ago."

"Yes. But that was different."

"I don't see how. M. St. Jacques is as much a gentleman as you are."

"Oh. Do you think so? But what about his head?"

For the instant, the Lady questioned the stability of Barth's own head.

"I really can't see how that enters into the question at all. Even a gentleman is liable to be hit on the head, when he is playing lacrosse."

"Lacrosse?"

"Yes. M. St. Jacques spent yesterday at Three Rivers with the lacrosse team from Laval."

"Oh." In his mortification at his own blunder, Barth's *oh* was more dissyllabic even than usual. "I didn't understand. I thought it was only the result of the banquet."

The Lady looked at him with a steady, kindly smile.

"Mr. Barth," she said; "I really think that idea was not quite worthy of you."

And Barth shut his lips in plucky acceptance of the rebuke.

The haunt of tourists and the prey of every artist, be his tools brushes or mere words, Sous-le-Cap remains the crowning joy of ancient Quebec. The inconsequent bends in its course, the wood flooring of its roadway, the crisscross network of galleries and verandas which join the two rows of houses and throw the street into a shadow still deeper than that cast by the overhanging cape, the wall of naked rock that juts out here and there between the houses piled helter-skelter against the base of the cliff: these details have endured for generations, and succeeding generations well may pray for their continued endurance. Quebec could far better afford to lose the whole ornate length of the Grand Allée than even one half the flying galleries and fluttering clothes-lines of little Sous-le-Cap.

"And yet," St. Jacques said thoughtfully; "this hardly makes me proud of my countrymen."

From the many-colored garments flapping on the clothes-lines, Nancy glanced down at a scarlet-coated child playing in the open doorway of a shop at her side.

"Don't think of the sociological aspect of the case," she advised him. "Once in a while, it is better to be simply picturesque than it is to be hygienic. I have seen a good deal of America; I know nothing to compare with this."

St. Jacques picked his way daintily among the rubbish.

"I hope not. I also hope there's not much in France."

"You have been there?" Nancy questioned.

"Not yet. After two more years at Laval."

"To live there?"

"Only to study. My home is here."

"Not in Quebec?"

"No. In Rimouski. I am a countryman," he added, with a smile.

"And shall you go back there?"

"It is impossible to tell. I hope not; but my father is growing older, and there are little children. In a case like that, one can never choose for himself," he said, with a little accent of regret.

"But your profession," Nancy reminded him. "Will there be any opening for it there?"

St. Jacques shrugged his shoulders.

"There is always an opening. It is only a question whether one feels too large to try to enter it. If I were as free as Mr. Brock, I would come back here, or go to The States. As it is, I am not free."

"Tell me about Rimouski," Nancy urged him.

"What do you care to know? It is a little place. The ocean-going steamers stop there; there is a cathedral and a seminary."

"Is it pretty?"

His eyes lighted.

"I was born there, Miss Howard. It is impossible for me to say. Perhaps sometime you may see it for yourself."

"I wish I might," the girl assented idly.

The next minute, she felt herself blushing, as she met the eager look on the face of her companion, and she hurried away from the dangerous subject.

"How long shall you be abroad?" she asked hastily.

"Two years."

"Nearly five years before you go into your professional work."

"Yes." His accent dropped a little. "It is long to wait."

"It depends on the way the time goes," Nancy suggested, with a fresh determination to drive the minor key from his voice. "Between banquets and lacrosse matches and broken heads, your days ought not to drag. Was it really so bad a bump you had?"

Pushing his cap still farther to the back of his head, St. Jacques lifted the dark hair from his forehead.

"So much," he said coolly, as he displayed a short, deep cut.

Nancy exclaimed in horror.

"M. St. Jacques! And you take it without a word of complaint."

This time, he laughed.

"Complaint never mends a split head, Miss Howard. We Frenchmen take our knocks and say nothing."

"Is that aimed at Mr. Barth?" Nancy asked.

St. Jacques shook his head; but his lips and eyes denied the gesture of negation.

"Really," she urged; "he didn't complain."

"No; but he talked about it more than I cared to listen."

"Aren't you a little hard on him, M. St. Jacques?"

The Frenchman looked up in surprise.

"Is he your friend, then?" he queried gravely.

"Yes. No. I don't know." Nancy was vainly struggling to frame her reply according to the strictest truth. "I think he thought so; but now we don't know."

"I am afraid I do not understand," St. Jacques said, with slow formality. "As your friend, I shall treat him with respect. Otherwise—"

"Oh, he isn't my friend," Nancy explained hurriedly. "We have had an awful fight; at least, not exactly a fight, but I was rude to him."

St. Jacques interrupted her.

"Then it will make up for some of the times he has been rude to me, and I shall be still more in your debt."

Nancy shook her head ruefully.

"No; we can't square our accounts that way, M. St. Jacques. I have seen Mr. Barth detestably rude to you, and it never once has dawned upon him that he wasn't the very pink of courtesy. With me, it was different. I did my very best, not only to be rude to him; but to have him know that I meant it."

Again came the answering flash over the Frenchman's face.

"I am very glad you did it," he said briefly.

"I'm not, then," Nancy said flatly. "I hate making apologies."

"Then let him apologize to you," St. Jacques suggested, laughing. "He has no right to put himself in the wrong so far as to make you feel it worth your while to be rude to him."

Nancy laughed in her turn.

"M. St. Jacques, you do not like Mr. Barth," she said merrily.

"No, Miss Howard; I do not. It will be a happy day for me, when he takes himself out to his ranch."

"But I shall have gone, long before that," she said thoughtfully.

St. Jacques turned upon her with a suddenness which startled her.

"So soon as that?"

"Sooner. Three or four weeks more here will see the end of our stay."

The blood rolled hotly upward across his swarthy face. Then it rolled back again, leaving behind it a pallor that brought his thin lips and resolute chin into strong relief.

"I am sorry," he said slowly. "I thought you had come to stay."

"Only till my father has ransacked every book in your Laval library," she said, with intentional lightness.

He declined to answer her tone. The words of his reply dropped, clear, distinct, slow, upon her ears.

"No matter. Perhaps some day you may come back to Canada, Miss Howard, come back, I mean, to stay."

Nancy drew two or three short, quick breaths. Then she laughed with a forced mirth.

"Perhaps. One can never tell. I like Canada," she said nervously.

St. Jacques faced her.

"And the Canadians?" he asked steadily.

His dark eyes held hers for a moment. Then she found herself repeating his words,—

"Yes, and the Canadians."

A moment later, she gave a sudden start of surprise and relief. Rounding a sharp angle in the winding street, they had found themselves directly upon the heels of Mr. Cecil Barth who was sauntering slowly along just ahead of them. Turning at the sound of their feet on the board roadway, he bowed to Nancy with deprecating courtesy, to her companion with studied carelessness.

Nancy's quick eye caught the veiled hostility of the salute exchanged by the two men. Her own poise was shaken by the little scene through which she had just been passing, but she made a desperate effort to regain control of the situation.

"Mr. Barth," she said impetuously.

Barth had resumed his stroll. At her words, he turned back instantly.

"Why not wait for us?" she suggested, as she held out her hand with frank cordiality. "M. St. Jacques deserves congratulations from us all, for his record at lacrosse, yesterday; and I know you'll like to add your voice to the general chorus. And, besides that, I owe you an apology. I was very rude to you, yesterday; but, at least, I have the saving grace to be thoroughly ashamed of myself, to-day."

And Barth, as he took her hand, felt that that minute atoned for many a bad half-hour she had given him in the past.

Together, they came out from under the hanging balconies, strayed on through Sault-au-Matelot and, coming up Mountain Hill Street, wandered out along the Battery. There they lingered to lean on the wall and stare across the river at the heights of Lévis bathed in its sunset light which is neither purple, nor yet altogether of gold. To Nancy, the light was typical of the hour. The girl was no egotist; yet all at once she instinctively realized that one or the other of these men was holding the key to her life. Which it should be, as yet she could not know. The hour had come, unsought, unexpected. For the present, it was better to drift. The mood of St. Jacques was kindred to her own. As for Barth, he was supremely content, without in the least knowing why his recent dissatisfaction should have fallen from him.

While they lingered by the wall, to watch the fading glow, Dr. Howard suddenly stepped out into the road behind them. As he came through the gate in the old stone wall, his glance rested upon the trio of familiar figures, and his voice rang out in hearty greeting.

"Well, Nancy," he called. "Are you watching for a hostile fleet?"

With the eagerness which never failed to welcome him, she turned to face her father; but, midway in her turning, she was stopped by Barth's voice.

"Nancy!" he echoed. "Are you another Nancy Howard?"

She faltered. Then she met his blue eyes full and steadily.

"No," she said, with fearless directness. "So far as I know, Mr. Barth, I am the only one."

CHAPTER FOURTEEN

With masculine obtuseness, Barth regarded it as a matter of pure chance that he found Nancy standing alone in the hall, that night.

"Please go away and take M. St. Jacques with you," she had begged Brock, as he had left the table. "I must have it out with him sometime, and I'd rather have it over."

Brock looked at his watch.

"Will an hour be long enough?" he asked.

"I can't tell. Please bid me good night now," she urged him.

He smiled reassuringly down into her anxious eyes.

"Don't take the situation too tragically, Miss Howard," he said, with a brotherly kindness she was quick to feel as a relief to her strained nerves. "You weren't to blame in the first place, and I can bear witness that you have been the most loyal friend he has had. If he is a bit unpleasant about it, send him to me, and I'll knock him down." He rose; but he lingered long enough to add, "I'll look in on you, about nine o'clock, and see if I can help pick up the pieces." And, with a nod of farewell, he was gone.

"Are you busy?" Barth asked, as he joined her, a little later.

"Am I ever busy in this indolent atmosphere?" she questioned in return, with a futile effort for her usual careless manner.

"Sometimes, as far as I am concerned. But what if we come into the drawing-room? It is quieter there."

He spoke gently, yet withal there was something masterful in his manner, and Nancy felt that her hour was come. Nervously she tried to anticipate it.

"And you need a quiet place for the scene of the fray?" she asked flippantly.

"Fray?" His accent was interrogative.

"For the discussion, then."

He was moving a chair forward. Then he looked up sharply, as he stood aside for her to take it.

"I can't see that there is reason for any discussion, Miss Howard."

"But you know you think I have been playing a double game with you," Nancy broke out, in sudden irritation at his quiet.

His hands in his pockets, he walked across to the window and stood looking out. Then he turned to face Nancy.

"No. I am not sure that I do."

"You feel that I ought to have told you before?"

"It would have been a little fairer to me," he assented.

"I don't see why," she said defensively.

Barth raised his blue eyes to her face, and she repented her untruth.

"At least," she amended; "I don't see what difference it would have made."

"Perhaps not. Still, it isn't pleasant to be a stranger, and the one person outside a secret which concerns one's self most of all."

"No."

"I wish you had told me," he said thoughtfully. "It might have prevented some things that now I should like to forget."

"For instance?"

"For instance, the way I have told you details with which you were already familiar."

Nancy laughed nervously.

"And some with which I wasn't familiar at all," she added.

Barth's color rose to the roots of his hair, and he bit his lip. Then he answered, with the same level accent,—

"Yes. But even you must admit that my error was unintentional."

Nancy sat up straight in her deep chair.

"Even me!" she echoed stormily. "What do you mean, Mr. Barth?"

He met her angry eyes fearlessly, yet with perfect respect.

"Even you who were willing to take all the advantage of a complete stranger."

"But I took no advantage," she protested.

"No," he admitted, after a pause. "Perhaps it was forced upon you. However, you accepted it. Miss Howard," he paused again; "we Englishmen dislike to make ourselves needlessly ridiculous."

She started to interrupt him; but he gave her no opportunity.

"I was ridiculous. I can fancy how funny it all must have seemed to you: my meeting you here without recognizing you, my telling you over all my regard for my former nurse. Of course, I must have seemed an ass to you, and to Mr. Brock and Mr. St. Jacques, too, after you had told them."

This time, Nancy did interrupt him.

"Stop, Mr. Barth!" she said angrily. "Now you are the one who is unfair. I did tell Mr. Brock about our adventure at Sainte Anne-de-Beaupré; but it was when I first met him, when I had no idea that either of us would ever see you again. I told the adventure; but I used no names. You had been in the house for several days before Mr. Brock found out that you were my former patient, and he found it out then from your own lips. When he told M. St. Jacques, or whether he told him at all, I am unable to say. I do know that M. St. Jacques knew it; but, upon my honor, I have told no one but the Lady and Mr. Reginald Brock."

Bravely, angrily, she raised her eyes to his. Notwithstanding his former doubts, Barth believed her implicitly.

"Forgive my misunderstanding you, then," he said simply. "But why couldn't you have told me?"

"How could I?"

"I don't see why not."

"I am sorry," she said briefly. "It seemed to me out of the question."

"Even when we were introduced?" he urged.

"It was before that that you had refused to recognize me."

"When was that?"

"At the table, the first time you reappeared here," she said vindictively. "I did my best to speak to you then; but you tried to give me the impression that you had never seen me before."

Barth bowed in assent.

"I never had. You forget that my glasses were lost. You should be generous to a near-sighted man, Miss Howard, as you once were kind to a cripple. You might have given me another chance, when we were introduced."

"There was nothing to show you cared for it," Nancy returned curtly.

"And, even at Sainte Anne, you might have told me you were coming to Quebec," he went on. "You knew I was coming here; you might have given me the opportunity to call and thank you."

Impatiently Nancy clasped her hands and unclasped them.

"What is the use of arguing about it all?" she demanded restlessly. "You never could see the truth of it; no man could. I don't want to beg off and make excuses. I have been in a false position from the start. I never made it, nor even sought it. It all came from chance. Still, it has been impossible for me to get myself out of it; but truly, Mr. Barth," she looked up at him appealingly; "from the first hour I met you at Sainte Anne until to-day, I have never meant to be disloyal to you."

"Then why couldn't you have told me you had met me before?" he asked, returning to his first question with a curious persistency.

Nancy fenced with the question.

"But, strictly speaking, I had not met you."

Barth's eyes opened to their widest limit.

"Oh, really," he said blankly.

"No; not in any social sense. Nobody introduced us. I was just your nurse."

Suddenly, for the first time since the discovery of Nancy's identity, there flashed upon Barth's mind the thought of the guinea. He turned scarlet. Then he rallied.

"Miss Howard," he said slowly, as he took the chair at her side; "I am not sure you were the only one who has been placed in a false position."

The girl's irritation vanished, and she laughed.

"About the guinea? Perhaps we can cry quits, Mr. Barth. Still, your mistake was justifiable. You took me for a nurse."

"Yes. And so you were."

"Thank you for the implied compliment. But, I mean, for a hired nurse."

"Certainly. I did hire you. At least, I paid you wa—"

In mercy to his later reflections, Nancy cut him off in the midst of his phrase.

"Perhaps. We knew you wouldn't let me do it out of charity, so my father collected his usual fee in two ways."

Barth's glasses had fallen from his nose. Now, his eyes still on Nancy's face, he felt vaguely for the string.

"And you never received your money?"

Again the frosty accent came into Nancy's tone.

"Certainly not."

"Oh, what a beastly shame!" And, seizing his glasses, Barth stared at her in commiserating surprise.

For a short instant, Nancy longed to tweak the glasses from his nose. Then she laughed.

"As a rule, I don't nurse people for money, Mr. Barth," she said lightly.

"No? How generous you must be, Miss Howard!"

Was there ever a more maddening combination of manly simplicity and British bigotry, Nancy reflected impatiently. More and more she began to despair of making her position clear. Nevertheless, she went on steadily,—

"And, in fact, you were my one and only patient."

"That you have ever had, in all your professional life?"

"I never had any professional life," Nancy replied shortly.

Barth's face showed his increasing perplexity.

"But you are a nurse."

"No," Nancy answered in flat negation.

"You nursed me."

"After a fashion."

"What for?"

Again Nancy's impatience gave place to mirth.

"To cure you, of course."

"Rather! But I didn't mean that. We all know it, in fact; and you did it awfully well. But what made you—er—pick me out in the first place?"

"Pick you out?" This time, Nancy was the one to show perplexity.

"Yes. How did you happen to choose me for a patient?"

Nancy gasped at the new phase of the situation opened by Barth's words. In his British ignorance of American customs, did he think that she habitually wandered about the country, selecting attractive strangers to be the objects of her feminine ministrations?

"I didn't choose you," she said indignantly.

"Then, by George, how did you get me?" Mr. Cecil Barth queried, by this time too tangled in the web of mystery to select his words with care.

Nancy blushed; then she frowned; then she laughed outright.

"Mr. Barth," she said at last; "we are talking in two different languages. If we keep on, we shall end by needing an interpreter. This is the whole of my side of the story, so please listen. I am not a nurse. I am not anything but just a commonplace American girl who dances and who eats fish in Lent. My father is a doctor, and, even in New York, one knows his name. He came up here to rest and to gather materials for a monograph on the miracles of Sainte Anne-de-Beaupré, and I came with him. I always do go with him. We had been at Sainte Anne a little more than a week, when there was a pilgrimage. I had never seen a pilgrimage, so I went down to the church. As I was coming out afterwards, I saw some one fall. No one was near, except the pilgrim people; and they all lost their heads and fell to crowding and gesticulating. I was afraid you would be trodden on; and my father has always trained me what to do in emergencies, so I told the people to stand back. By the time I could get to you, you had fainted; but I saw you were no pilgrim. In fact," Nancy added, with sudden malice; "I took you for an American."

Barth winced.

"Oh, I am sure you were very kind," he protested hastily.

"I am glad you think so. Well, you know the rest of the story."

Barth rose and stood facing her.

"No," he objected. "That is exactly what I do not know."

"How you were taken to the Gagnier farm?"

"How you became my nurse," he persisted quietly. "Please don't leave that out of your story, Miss Howard."

She smiled.

"It was sheer necessity, Mr. Barth. You said you spoke no French; neither did I. You were suffering and in need of a doctor at once. I knew of no doctor there but my father, and you assented to my suggestion of him. He will tell you that your ankle was in a bad condition and needed constant care. I knew he was not strong enough to give it, and I telegraphed all over Quebec in a vain search for a nurse. I couldn't get one; neither, for the sake of a few conventions, could I let you end your days with a stiff ankle. There was only one thing to be done, and I did it." She stopped for a moment. Then she added, "I only hope I may not have done it too clumsily. It was new work for me, Mr. Barth; but I did the very best I could."

In her earnest self-justification, she sat looking up at Barth with the unconscious eyes of a child. Barth held out his hand.

"Miss Howard, you must have thought me an awful cad," he said contritely.

"I did, at first; but now I know better," she answered honestly. "There was no real reason you should have known I was not an hireling. At first, I resented it, though. I resented it again, when you came here and didn't recognize me. It seemed to me impossible that you could have spent ten days with me, and forgotten me so completely. It wasn't flattering to my vanity, Mr. Barth; and I only gained my lost self-respect when you informed me, the other day, that you were still hoping to meet me again."

He echoed her laugh; but his tone was a little eager, as he added,—

"And that, in my secret thoughts, I used to call you my Good Sainte Anne?"

Nancy shook her head.

"Never that, I fear," she answered lightly. "The Good Sainte Anne works miracles, Mr. Barth."

"Oh, yes," he said slowly. "I know she does. But sometimes the surest miracles are the slowest to reach their full perfection."

"And there are many pilgrims to her shrine who go away again without having beheld a miracle," she reminded him, still with the same lightness.

"Oh, rather!" he answered gravely. "Still, do you know, Miss Howard, I may be the one exception who proves the rule."

CHAPTER FIFTEEN

"And what next?" Brock inquired, the next morning.

"Market," Nancy replied.

"To spend your guinea?"

"Hush!" she bade him, with a startled glance over her shoulder.

"Oh, you needn't worry. Barth never gets around till the fifty-ninth minute. He'll wait until the last trump sounds, before he orders his ascension robe, and then he'll tip Saint Peter to hold the gate open while he puts it on. But what about the market?"

"I am going with the Lady."

"To carry the basket?"

"No. I'll leave that for you," Nancy retorted.

A sudden iniquitous idea shot athwart Brock's brain.

"Very well. What time do you start?"

"At ten."

"Right, oh! I'll be on hand."

An equally iniquitous idea entered Nancy's head.

"Have you ever been to market?" she asked.

"Never."

"And you want to go?"

"Surely I do."

"Then we can count on you?"

"Yes. Ten o'clock sharp. If I'm not there, I'll agree to send a substitute. But count on me."

When they went their separate ways from breakfast, Brock sought the town house of the Duke of Kent; but Nancy went in search of the Lady.

"Were you going to take Tommy to carry the basket?" she asked.

"Yes. He always goes."

"And will the basket be very huge?"

"Yes."

"Good!" Nancy said, laughing. "I am glad, for we are going to leave Tommy at home, to-day, and take Mr. Brock in his place."

"Nancy!" the Lady remonstrated.

"He insisted upon being invited," Nancy returned obdurately; "and, if he does go, he must be made useful. We sha'n't need both him and Tommy; Mr. Brock wants to carry the basket."

Brock, meanwhile, had left the maid standing in the lower hallway and, two steps at a time, was mounting the ducal staircase which led to Barth's room. His fist, descending upon the panels, cleft the Englishman's dream in two.

"Oh, yes. What is it? Wait a bit, and I'll let you in."

From the other side of the door, muffled sounds betrayed the fact that Barth was struggling with his dressing-gown and slippers. Then the door was flung open, and Barth stood on the threshold. He started back in astonishment, as he caught sight of his unexpected guest.

"Oh. Mr. Brock?"

"Yes. Sorry to have routed you out so early; but I came to bring you word from Miss Howard and the Lady."

Barth stepped away from the doorway.

"Come in," he said hospitably. "Excuse the look of the place, though."

Brock's keen eyes swept the room with direct, impersonal curiosity, took note of the half-unpacked boxes, the piles of books, the heaps of clothing, then moved back to Barth's face, where they rested with mirthful, kindly scrutiny. Then he crossed the room and dropped into a chair by the window.

"You brought me a message from Miss Howard?" Barth queried tentatively, after a pause which his companion seemed disinclined to break.

"Not so much a message as a—a suggestion," Brock answered, with a hesitation so short as to escape the Englishman's ear. "Miss Howard and the Lady are going to market, this morning, and I gathered, from what Miss Howard said, that she would like you to be on hand."

"To—market?"

"Yes. She evidently thought you understood it was an engagement. The only question seemed to be about the hour."

"Oh. What time do they go?"

"Ten."

"And now?"

"It is past nine now."

Barth stepped to the table and glanced at his watch.

"Fifteen past nine," he read. "There is plenty of time. And you are sure Miss Howard wanted me?"

"Perfectly," Brock answered, with brazen mendacity.

"How strange!" observed Mr. Cecil Barth.

"Strange that she should want you? Oh, not at all," Brock demurred politely.

"Oh, no. Strange that she shouldn't have mentioned it before."

"Didn't she say anything about it, last night?" Brock inquired.

"No. At least, I don't remember it."

"It may have slipped her mind. You had a good deal to talk over, I believe."

"What do people do, when they go to market?" Barth queried, with sudden and intentional inconsequence.

"Buy things."

"Yes. But what sort of things?"

"Haven't you been down into the market yet?" Brock asked, as he craned his neck to watch two girls passing in the street beneath.

"Oh, no. Why should I?"

"Strangers generally do; it is quite one of the sights."

"Do you mind if I begin dressing, Mr. Brock? What sort of sights?"

"Oh, cabbages, and pigs, and country things like that."

Barth's brows knotted, partly over his dressing, partly over his effort to grasp the situation.

"And is Miss Howard going down to—to look at those things?" he inquired.

"No, man; of course not. She is going down with the Lady to buy them."

"To—buy—a pig?" Barth spoke in three detached sentences.

Brock smothered his merriment according to the best of his ability.

"The Lady will do the buying. Miss Howard goes to look on."

"And does she expect me to look on, too?"

"Certainly."

Barth sat with his shoe horn hanging loosely in his hand.

"But, Mr. Brock, I don't know a bad pig from a good one," he protested hastily.

"Oh, it's quite easy to tell. Just pinch him a bit about the ribs. If he is fat and squeals nicely, he'll go. But, as I understand it, you aren't to do the marketing. You are expected to carry the basket for them."

Barth looked up from his second shoe.

"The basket?"

"Yes. Women here take their baskets with them."

"And get them filled?"

"Surely. Then they bring them home."

Barth finished the tying of his shoestrings. Then he rose and picked up his collar.

"Oh, really!" he remonstrated, as he fumbled with the buttonholes. "Miss Howard can't be expecting that I am going to bring a pig home in my arms."

Brock rose.

"It is never safe to predict what a pretty woman will expect next," he said oracularly. "I usually make a point of being ready for almost anything. As far as Miss Howard is concerned, I'd rather carry a pig for her than a bunch of roses for some women."

This time, Brock's words rang true. Moreover, they dismissed any doubts lingering in the mind of his companion.

"Oh, rather!" he assented, with some enthusiasm.

A mocking light came into Brock's clear eyes.

"I am glad you agree with me. You knew her before I did, I believe."

"Yes. At Sainte Anne-de-Beaupré. Miss Howard was very good to me, when I was there." Over the top of his half-fastened collar, Barth spoke with simple dignity.

Brock liked the tone.

"I can imagine it, Barth," he answered, with a sudden wave of liking for the loyal little Englishman before him. "Both St. Jacques and I would gladly have offered up our ankles at the shrine of Sainte Anne, for such a chance as yours."

"What kind of a chance do you mean?"

"Chance to be coddled by Miss Howard, of course."

Barth slid the string of his glasses over his head, put on his glasses and looked steadily up at Brock.

"It was a chance," he assented gravely. "Chance and the handiwork of the Good Sainte Anne. It might have meant a good deal to me. Instead, I threw it all away by my own dulness; and now, instead of having the advantage of a three-weeks' acquaintance, I have to start at the very beginning once more. If, as you are hinting, you and Mr. St. Jacques and I are on a strife to win the regard of Miss Howard, you and Mr. St. Jacques have already distanced me in the race."

Brock laughed; but his eyes had grown surprisingly gentle. In all his easy-going life, a life when friends and their confidences had been his for the asking, few things had touched him as did this direct, simple expression of trust on the part of Mr. Cecil Barth. Contrary to his custom, he met confidence with confidence.

"You're a good fellow, Barth," he said heartily. "I am a little out of the running, myself. I'd like to wish you success, if I could; but St. Jacques is the older friend." Then, relenting, he recurred to the object of his call. "Now see here, Barth," he added; "you needn't feel obliged to go to market. There may be some joke in the matter. Miss Howard laughed, when she was talking about it. Don't go, if you don't wish to. They can take Tommy."

"Oh, but I'd like to go," Barth interposed hurriedly, as he looked at his watch. "It is past ten now, Mr. Brock. May I ask you to excuse me?" And, without waiting for a final word from Brock, he turned and went dashing down the staircase at a speed which boded little good for an invalid ankle.

Ten o'clock, that sunny morning, found Champlain Market the centre of an eager, jostling, basket-laden throng. As a rule, the Lady sought her purchases at the market just outside the Saint John Gate. To-day, however, she had elected to go to the Lower Town, and, true to an old engagement, Nancy had elected to go with her. It was a novel experience for the girl, and she wandered up and down at the heels of the Lady, now staring at the stout old habitant women who, since early dawn, had sat wedged into their packed carts, knitting away as comfortably as if they had been surrounded by sofa pillows rather than by pumpkins; at the round-faced, bundled-up children who guarded the stalls of belated flowers, of blue-yarn socks and of baskets of every size; at the groups of men, gathered here and there in the throng, offering to their possible customers the choice between squealing pigs and squawking fowls which one and all seemed to be resenting the liberties taken with their breast-bones. Back of the old stone market building, the carts were drawn up in long lines; and the board platforms between were heaped with cabbages and paved with crates. At the north, the little gray spire of Notre Dame des Victoires guarded the square where, for over two hundred years, it had done honor to the name of Our Lady and to the memory of successive victories won, by her protecting care, over invading foes. Above it all, the black-faced cannon poked its sullen nose over the wall of the King's Bastion where, a scarlet patch against the sky, there fluttered the threefold cross of the Union Jack.

And still Brock failed to appear.

"Just like a man!" Nancy said impatiently, as the half-hour struck. "You are sure Mary understood the message?"

"She never forgets. I was sorry not to wait, Nancy; but we should have lost our chance to get anything good. We are late, as it is."

"Late! What time does the market open?"

"By five o'clock. These people have been coming in, all night long. By five in the morning, the place is full of customers. It is worth the seeing then."

Nancy shivered.

"Uh! Not at this season of the year. I am not fond of the clammy dawn; and, down here by the river, it must be deathly. But, in the meanwhile,—" Again she glanced towards the corner of Little Champlain Street.

The Lady laughed.

"It is no use, Nancy. You are caught in your own trap, and now you must either go home and send Tommy to me, or else help me to carry home the basket."

"I don't mind the basket, though I confess I wish I hadn't urged you to bring your very largest one. But I am disappointed in Mr. Brock. I thought he possessed more invention than this. He made me believe he had some mischief lurking in his brain; and it is very flat and boyish merely to promise to appear and then not to materialize."

"He may have been prevented, at the last minute."

"Then," Nancy responded grimly; "he'd much better have kept to the letter of his promise and sent a substitute."

She was still wandering aimlessly to and fro among the crowd, now jostled by a packed basket on the arm of a sturdy habitant, now whacked on the ankle by a hen dangling limply, head downward, from the hand of the habitant's wife, now pausing to bargain for a bunch of pale violet sweet peas or a tiny replica of one of the melon-shaped baskets so characteristic of the town. All at once, she turned to the Lady.

"If there isn't Mr. Barth!" she exclaimed, lapsing, in her surprise, into the unmistakable vernacular of The States.

The Lady was deeply absorbed in her final purchase of the day, which, as it chanced, was a piglet for the morrow's dinner. Engrossed in the relative merits of a whole series of piglets of varying dimension, she was deaf to Nancy's words. Left to herself, the girl met Barth with an eager smile.

"Is it peace, or war?" she asked merrily, as she gave him her hand, sweet peas and all.

"Peace, of course. Are the flowers a token of the treaty?"

"Do you want them?"

"Oh, rather!" And Barth pulled off his glove to fasten them into the lapel of his dark blue coat. "I am so sorry to be late, Miss Howard; but Mr. Brock stopped a little, to talk."

"You have seen Mr. Brock, this morning?"

"Oh, yes. He was in my room."

Nancy's face betrayed her surprise.

"And did he say anything about market?"

"He told me you were coming at ten. I meant to be on hand; but he delayed me, and, when I finally started, I missed my way and came out over by the custom house. I must have taken a wrong turning."

"Perhaps. But where is Mr. Brock?"

"I think he went to his office."

There was a little pause.

"Jolly crowd, this," Barth commented at length. "Where is the Lady?"

"Over there." Nancy pointed to the Lady, still bending over the crate of piglets.

"Oh. And those are the pigs? Oughtn't we to go across and help her?"

Nancy laughed.

"I am afraid I'm not a judge of them," she demurred.

Barth's voice dropped confidentially.

"Neither am I. Still, as long as I came to help her, I think it would be rather decent to see if I can do anything about it, now I am here."

"Oh," Nancy said blankly. "Was the Lady expecting you?"

Barth's gratified smile completed her mystification.

"Oh, rather! I wouldn't have felt at liberty without, you know. That's what the Lady is for."

A moment later, the Lady started in surprise. Stick and gloves in hand and a frown of deep consideration on his boyish brow, Barth suddenly knelt down at her side and shut his slim fingers upon the flank of the nearest piglet, which gave vocal expression to its displeasure.

"Oh. Good morning," he added, not to the piglet, however, but to the Lady. "I think you will find this little chap quite satisfactory."

For an instant, Nancy had difficulty in repressing her mirth. Then, from the Lady's manifest astonishment at Barth's appearing, from Barth's own manner, and from her memory of Brock's final words, she saw the hand of the young Canadian in the situation. This was the substitute whom Brock had promised. She determined to put her theory to the test.

"Mr. Brock was very good to act as our messenger," she suggested craftily.

"Rather! He is a good fellow, anyway," Barth answered, as he rose and dusted off his knees. "I like the English Canadians, myself. They are a grade above the French ones. But, do you know, Mr. Brock only just saved me from disgracing myself again. I was so absorbed in—in the other things we talked over, last night, that I quite forgot about the trip to market, this morning."

For a minute, as she looked into Barth's animated face, Nancy waxed hot with indignation over Brock's childish trick. She half resolved to warn the young Englishman against the species of hazing which he was called upon to undergo. Then she held her peace. Her warnings would count for more, if she levelled them at Brock, rather than at Brock's victim. Even her limited experience of Barth had assured her that, in certain directions, his understanding was finite. It would never occur to his insular mind that his very naïveté would make him a more tempting prey to the jovial young Canadian.

"Never mind, as long as you came at all, Mr. Barth," she replied lightly. "It would have been a pity for you to have missed the sight. We couldn't very well wait for you, because the Lady had to come on business, not pleasure."

"And is this all?" Barth said, as the Lady turned from the piglet. "Where is the basket?"

"There." And Nancy, as she pointed to the heaped assortment of garden stuffs, suddenly resolved to put Barth's chivalry to the test.

The test was weighty, unlovely of outline and unsavory of odor; nevertheless, the young Britisher did not shrink. Without a glance around him, Mr. Cecil Barth bent over the great basket and passed its handles over the curve of his elbow.

"Shall we go home by the steps?" he asked. "Or do you take the lift?"

Then the Lady interfered.

"I go to the nearest cab-stand," she replied promptly. "I find I must dash over to the other market as fast as I can go. There are cabs just around the corner, Mr. Barth, if you are willing to put my basket into one. Then, if you and Miss Howard will excuse me for deserting the expedition, I will leave you to walk home together."

And Nancy's answering smile assured the Lady of her full forgiveness.

CHAPTER SIXTEEN

"I love all things British, saving and excepting their manners and their mortar," Nancy soliloquized.

Nancy's temper was ruffled, that morning. As she had left the table, Barth had followed her to the parlor where, apparently apropos of an inoffensive Frenchman crossing the Place d'Armes, he had been drawn into strictures concerning American and French peculiarities of speech and manner. The talk had been impersonal; nevertheless, Nancy had been quick to discern that its text lay in the growing friendship between herself and St. Jacques. For a time, she had listened in silence to the Britisher's accusing monologue. Then her temper had given way completely. Flapping the American flag full in his face, she had loosed the American eagle and promptly routed Barth and driven him from the field, with the British Lion trudging dejectedly at his heels.

"I want him to understand that he's not to say *American* to me, in any such tone as that!" Nancy muttered vindictively, as she pinned on her hat.

Then she went out to walk herself into a good temper.

The good temper was still conspicuous by its absence, when, regardless of appearances, she dropped down in the grass by the hospital gate, and fell to picking the scraps of mortar out of the meshes of her rough cloth gown.

"I believe I am all kinds of an idiot," she continued to herself explosively. "First, Joe's letter rubbed me the wrong way. I don't see how he could be so stupid as to imagine I'm homesick. Of course, I am glad he is coming up here; but an extra man, in any relation, does have a tendency to complicate things. And then Mr. Brock didn't come to breakfast. I know he was cross, last night, because I took Mr. Barth's part. And now Mr. Barth has made me lose my temper again. I believe he does it, just for the sake of seeing me abase myself afterwards. Dear me! Everybody is cross, and I am the crossest of the lot."

Beside her on the grass, the shadow of the Union Jack above the hospital moved idly to and fro. Behind her was the low, squat bulk of the third Martello Tower whose crumbling mortar Nancy was even now removing from her clothing. The fourth Martello Tower, hidden somewhere within the dingy confines of Saint Sauveur, had eluded all her efforts to find it; the other two had been too obviously converted to twentieth-century purposes. This had looked more inviting, and Nancy had spent a chilly hour in its depths. By turning her back upon the dripping icehouse in its southern edge, and focussing her mind upon the mammoth central column which supported its arching roof, she had been able to force herself backward into the days when a Martello Tower was a thing for an invading army to reckon with. In the magazine beneath, the drip from the icehouse had spoiled the illusion; but the open platform above, albeit now snugly roofed in, still offered its battlements and its trio of dismounted cannon to her cynical gaze. Nancy left the dim interior, bored, but sternly just. In some moods and with certain companions, even the third Martello Tower might be interesting. Meantime, she was conscious of a distinct wish that the relics of the crumbling past might not have such marked affinity for her shoulder-blades.

"Miss Howard!"

She looked up. Cap in hand, St. Jacques was standing before her.

"I am glad I have found you," he added directly. "I was wishing that something good might happen."

Nancy's smile broadened to a laugh.

"Are you cross, too?" she queried, without troubling herself to rise.

"Very," St. Jacques assented briefly.

"I am so glad. Let's be cross together."

"Here?"

"Why not?"

The Frenchman shrugged his shoulders.

"I don't like the place. The associations are not pleasant."

"I don't see why. It looks a very comfortable place to be ill."

"Yes; but who wants to think of being ill?"

"Nobody," Nancy returned philosophically. "Still, now and then we must, you know. Witness Mr. Barth."

St. Jacques smiled.

"Yes. But even Mr. Barth had a good nurse."

"Don't be too sure of that. Even my level best is none too even," Nancy replied enigmatically, with scant consideration for the alien tongue of her companion.

He ignored her words.

"If I should be ill, would you take care of me?" he asked suddenly.

Still laughing, the girl shook her head.

"Never. I like you altogether too well, M. St. Jacques, to risk your life with my ministrations. Instead of that, though, I will come out here to see you as often as you will grant me admission."

"Not here. They would never grant me admission in the first place," St. Jacques responded dryly.

"Why, then?"

"Because I am Catholic."

"Oh, how paltry!" Nancy burst out in hot indignation.

"It is true, however."

With a sweep of her arm, Nancy pointed to the Union Jack whose scarlet folds stained the sky line.

"Then the sooner they pull that down, the better," she said scornfully. "I thought that the British flag stood for religious freedom."

"But you are not Catholic," St. Jacques said slowly.

"What difference does that make? I am not a Seven-Day Baptist, either. Neither fact makes me ignore the rights of my friends who are."

St. Jacques still stood looking down at her. His face was unusually grave, that morning; and it seemed to Nancy that his swarthy cheeks were flushed more than it was their wont to be.

"You have friends who are Catholics?" he asked.

"One, I hope," she answered quietly. Then she rose to her feet. "What are you doing out here at this hour?" she added.

"Walking, to tire myself," he answered. "Will you come?"

For her only answer, she dropped into step at his side, and they turned down the steep slope leading into Saint Sauveur, crossed Saint Roch and the Dorchester Bridge and came out on the open road to Beauport.

Never a garrulous companion, St. Jacques was more silent than ever, that morning, and Nancy let him have his way. Moreover, at times she was conscious of something restful in the long pauses which came in her talk with St. Jacques. When he chose, the young Frenchman spoke easily and well. Apparently, however, he saw no need of talking, unless he had something to say. In their broken talk and their long silences, Nancy had gained a better understanding of St. Jacques, a more perfect sympathy with his point of view and his mood than she had gained of Brock in all their hours of chattering intercourse.

For a long mile, they walked on without speaking. Shoulder to shoulder, they had gone tramping along the narrow plank walk with the sure rhythm of perfectly adapted step.

"How well we walk together!" Nancy said, suddenly breaking the silence.

"Yes," St. Jacques assented briefly. "I have always noticed it."

Some men would have used her random words as the theme for a sentimental speech. To St. Jacques, they were too obvious; emotion should not be wasted upon anything so matter of fact. Long since, Nancy had become accustomed to that phase of his mind. It gave a certain restfulness to their intercourse to know that St. Jacques would never read unintended meanings into her simplest utterances. At first, she had supposed him too stolid, too earnestly intent upon his own ends to waste sentiment upon herself. Lately, she had begun to doubt; and she confessed to herself that the doubt was sweet.

"You said you were cross, to-day?" St. Jacques broke the silence, this time.

"Yes, detestably."

"For any especial reason?"

"How uncomplimentary of you to suggest that I am ever cross without reason!" Nancy rebuked him.

"What is the reason?" he asked coolly.

"There are several of them, all tangled up together."

"And, as usual, Barth is one of them," St. Jacques supplemented.

"Perhaps; and Mr. Brock is another," Nancy replied unexpectedly.

"Brock? What has he done?"

"Nothing. I did it. At least, I tried to lecture him for playing tricks on Mr. Barth, and—"

"One is always at liberty to play tricks with a monkey," St. Jacques interpolated quietly.

"Mr. Barth isn't a monkey," Nancy retorted.

"No? Then what is he?"

"The best little Englishman that ever lived," she answered promptly.

The lower lip of St. Jacques rolled out into his odd little smile.

"Then the game surely ought to be in the hands of the French," he responded.

"You're not fair to Mr. Barth," Nancy said, as she stooped to pull off a spray of scarlet maple leaves from a bush at her feet.

"Perhaps not. Neither are you."

"Yes, I am. He hasn't a more loyal friend in America, M. St. Jacques."

"I know that. It is not always fair to be too loyal."

"Why not?"

"Because it makes one wonder whether the game is worth the candle," the Frenchman replied imperturbably. "One doesn't fly to defend the strongest spot on the city wall."

Nancy looked up into his dark face.

"No; and, in the same way, I've not fought a battle in your behalf since we met."

"No?"

"At least—" she added hurriedly, as she recalled stray sentences of her talk with Barth, that morning. "But in a way you have told the truth. I have fought Mr. Barth's battles with you all, until I sometimes feel as if I were wholly responsible for the man."

"Then why not let him fight his own battles?"

A torn red leaf fluttered from Nancy's fingers.

"Because he won't. It's not that he is a coward; it's not that he is conceited or too sure of himself. It is only that he is like a great, overgrown child who never stops to think of the impression he is making. Sometimes it is refreshing; sometimes it makes one long to box him up and send him back to be tethered out on a chain attached to Westminster Abbey. Even that wouldn't do, though, for the Poets' Corner has made room for an American or two. Mr. Barth is queer and innocent and, just now and then, superlatively stupid. And yet, M. St. Jacques, I don't believe he ever had an ignoble idea from the day of his birth up to to-day. He is absolutely generous and high-minded, and one can forgive a good deal for the sake of that."

Flushed with her eager championship, she paused and smiled up into her companion's eyes. His answering smile drove the gravity from his face.

"Yes," he assented; "and, from your very persistence, you imply that there is a good deal to forgive."

"Something, perhaps," she assented in her turn; "but it is largely negative. Meanwhile, he isn't fair game for you and Mr. Brock."

"Why not?"

"Because he believes everything you tell him; because it never once enters his mind that you would find it worth your while to torment him. If he lets you alone, he expects you to do the same by him."

St. Jacques made no answer. With his dark eyes fixed on the broad river at his right hand, he marched steadily along by Nancy's side until the quaint little roadside cross of temperance was far behind them. Then he said abruptly,—

"Miss Howard, I wish I knew just how well you like that fellow."

Nancy's thoughts, like her steps, had lain parallel to his. She responded now without hesitation,—

"I wish I knew, myself; but I don't."

For an instant, St. Jacques removed his eyes from the river. He smiled, as he moved them back again.

Nancy's next words showed that her mind had taken a backward leap.

"You said you were walking to tire yourself?" she said interrogatively.

"Yes. Am I also tiring you?" St. Jacques answered, with instant courtesy.

"No. I always dislike the turning around to go home by the same road."

"Then we can walk on to Beauport church, and take the tram back," he suggested.

"As you like," she agreed. "But why tire yourself?"

The thin, firm lips shut into a resolute line. Then St. Jacques replied briefly,—

"I have been lying awake too much for my pleasure."

"Thinking of your sins?" Nancy asked gayly.

"Yes, and of some other things."

"Pleasant things, I hope."

The Frenchman's brows contracted.

"I have had dreams that were pleasanter."

Nancy stole a sidelong glance at him, saw the expression in his eyes, and, turning, looked him full in the face.

"M. St. Jacques," she said quietly; "something is wrong."

He smiled, as he shook his head; but his eyes did not light.

"There is no use of denying it. I have been a nurse, you know," she persisted laughingly; "and I have learned to watch for symptoms. Men don't frown like that and beetle their brows, without some cause or other. Does something worry you; or aren't you feeling well?"

Without breaking his even pace, St. Jacques turned and looked steadily into her earnest, sympathetic face. This time, his dark eyes lighted in response to the friendly look in her own.

"Perhaps it may be a little of both," he answered quietly. "Even then, there is no reason one should be a worry to one's friends."

The pause which followed was a short one. Then St. Jacques roused himself and laughed.

"Really, Miss Howard," he added, as he brushed his thick hair backward from the scarlet gash in his forehead; "it is only that I started with headache, this morning. I was too dull for work; but either Nurse Howard or the Good Sainte Anne has made me forget it."

And Nancy smiled back at him in token of perfect understanding. She had not heard his last inaudible words,—

"Or perhaps it may be the work of good Saint Joseph."

In fact, Nancy Howard as yet had gained no inkling of the especial attributes of Saint Joseph, nor did she suspect the part that the good old saint was beginning to play in the coming events of her life. To Nancy's mind, May was always May. So long as it lasted, there was no reason for looking forward into the coming month of June. The future tense was created solely for those whose present was not absolutely good.

CHAPTER SEVENTEEN

Confronted by a tea-tray and a Britisher in combination, Nancy Howard was conscious of a certain abashment.

At home in New York, she was accustomed to administer informal tea by means of a silver ball and a spirit lamp. These two diminutive pots, the one of water and the other of tea, left her in a blissful state of uncertainty whether she was to measure them out, half and half, or, emptying the teapot at the first round, fill it up with the water in the hopes of decocting a feeble second cup. Moreover, Nancy preferred lemon in her tea, and, worst of all, there were no sugar tongs. Nancy wondered vaguely whether Englishwomen were wont to make tea in brand-new gloves, or whether Englishmen were less finical than their transatlantic brethren.

Barth, his glasses on his nose, watched her intently. His very intentness increased her abashment. It had been at his suggestion that they had gone to the little tea shop, that afternoon, and Nancy had no wish to bring disgrace either upon Barth or herself, in the presence of those of Quebec's fair daughters who, at the tables around them, were sipping tea and gossip by turns.

Devoutly praying that she might not upset the cream jug, nor forget to call the sugarbowl a *basin*, Nancy at last succeeded in filling Barth's cup.

"How scriptural!" he observed, as he took it from her hand.

"In what way?"

He pointed to the pale ring of overflow in the saucer.

"It runneth over," he quoted gravely.

Nancy developed a literal turn of mind. She did it now and then; it was always unexpected, and it left her companion of the moment in the conversational lurch.

"That means happiness, not tea," she said calmly.

Barth looked at her inquiringly. Then, with unwonted swiftness, he rallied.

"Sometimes the two are synonymous," he said quietly.

But Nancy turned wayward.

"Not when they are watered down. But you must admit that Americans give good measure."

Barth smiled across the table at her, in manifest content.

"Of both," he asserted, as he stirred his tea.

"Have a biscuit," Nancy advised him suddenly.

"A—Would you like me to order some? I dare say they have them out there."

Nancy rested her elbows on the table with a protesting bump.

"There you go Britishing me again!" she said hotly. "You said you wouldn't do it. Even if I am an American, I do know enough not to say *cracker*. That was one of the few lessons I learned at my mother's knee. But there aren't any cracker-biscuits here. I was referring to these others."

Barth glanced anxiously about the table. Aside from the tray, there were two plates upon the table, and one of the two held tiny strips of toasted bread. All told, there were exactly eight of the strips, each amounting to a mouthful and a half, and Nancy had just been out at the Cove Fields, playing golf.

Nancy pointed to the other plate.

"I mean those—biscuits," she said conclusively and with emphasis.

"Those? Oh. But those aren't biscuits."

"What do you call them, then? Buns?" Nancy inquired, with scathing curiosity.

"Buns? Oh, no. Those are scones."

This time, Nancy fairly bounced in her chair.

"They are nothing in this world but common, every-day American soda biscuits," she said, as she helped herself to the puffiest and the brownest. "You are in America now, Mr. Barth, and there is no sense in your putting British names to our cooking. Will you have a biscuit?"

"Oh, yes. But really, you know, they are scones," he protested. "My mother nearly always has them."

Nancy cast anxious eyes at the drop of molten butter that was trickling along the base of her thumb.

"And so do we," she replied firmly; "only we eat them at breakfast, with a napkin. I don't mean that we actually eat the napkin," she explained hastily, in mercy for the limitations of her companion's understanding. "But, really, these are very buttery."

Barth sucked his forefinger with evident relish.

"Oh, rather!" he assented. "That's what makes them so good."

Nancy furtively rescued her handkerchief from her temporary substitute for a pocket. Then, bending forward, she arranged four of the strips of toast around the margin of her saucer.

"What's that for?" Barth queried, at a loss to know whether the act was another Americanism, or merely a Nancyism pure and simple.

"We are going to go halves on our rations," Nancy answered coolly. "I am just as hungry as you are, and I don't propose to have you eating more than your share of things."

"Would you like to have me order some more scones?" he asked courteously.

For the space of a full minute, Nancy bestowed her entire attention upon her teacup. Then she lifted the white of one eye to Barth's questioning face.

"Oh, rather!" she responded nonchalantly.

At the tables around them, Quebec's fair daughters paused in their tea and their gossip to cast a questioning glance in the direction of Barth's mirth. As a rule, masculine mirth had scant place in the cosy little tea shop. In summer, it was visited by a procession of American tourists who imbibed its tea in much the same solemn spirit as they breathed the incense of the Basilica, inhaled the crisp breeze over Cape Diamond and tasted the vigorous brew that ripened in the vaults of the old intendant's palace. When the tourists had betaken themselves southward and Quebec once more began to resume its customary life, the shop became a purely feminine function. It was an ideal place for a dish of gossip in the autumnal twilight. The walls hung thick with ancient plates and mirrors, venerable teapots and jugs stood in serried ranks along the shelf about the top of the room, and a quaint assortment of rugs nearly covered the floor. Here and there about the wide room were scattered little claw-footed tables whose shiny tops were covered with squares of homespun linen, brown and soft as a bit of Indian pongee. Not even the blazing electric lights could give an air of modernness to the place, and Nancy, in the intervals of her struggles with the tray, looked about her with complete content.

Barth possessed certain of the attributes of a successful general. Wide experience had taught him to administer fees freely and, as a rule, with exceeding discretion. As a result, he and Nancy were in possession of the most desirable table in the room, close beside the deep casement overlooking Saint Louis Street. Nancy, the light falling full on her eager face, over her radiant hair and on her dark cloth gown, could watch at her will the loitering passers in the street beneath, or the idle groups at the tables around her. Barth, his own face in shadow, could see but one thing. That one thing, however, was quite enough, for it was Nancy.

More than a week had passed since the morning in the market. To Mr. Cecil Barth, the week had seemed like a year, and yet shorter than many a single day of his past experience. Their walk homeward from the market had been by way of Saint Roch and the old French fortifications, and their conversation had been as devious as their path. Nevertheless, Barth, as he sat in his room applying liniment and red flannel to his aching ankle, felt that they had been moving straight towards a perfect understanding and good-fellowship. He had left Nancy, the night before, convinced of her generosity, but equally convinced that the worst hour of his life had been the hour when he took the train for Sainte Anne-de-Beaupré. Now, as he meditatively contemplated the pool of liniment on the carpet at his feet, he acknowledged to himself that the Good Sainte Anne had wrought a mighty series of miracles in his behalf, and he offered up a prayer, as devout as it was incoherent, that she might not remove her favor until she had wrought the mightiest miracle of all. Then, his prayer ended and his ankle anointed, he fell to whistling contentedly to himself as he tied up his shoe and brushed his yellow hair in preparation for dinner.

As far as possible, for the next week, he had been a fixture at Nancy's side. As yet, much walking was out of the question for him; but, within the narrow limits of the city wall, or under the roof of The Maple Leaf, neither Brock nor St. Jacques were able to sever him from his self-imposed connection with Nancy's apron string. He took small part in the conversation; with Brock, at least, he manifested a complete indifference to the course of events. It was merely that he was there, and that there he meant to stay, filling in the hiatuses of Nancy's time, answering her lightest appeals for attention and now and then adding a pithy word of support to even her most wayward opinions. It was not the first time that an invading British force had encamped about a fortress at Quebec. Wolfe at the head of his army showed no more gritty determination to win than did that quiet, simple-minded Britisher, Mr. Cecil Barth.

And, as the October days crept by, Nancy Howard grew increasingly nervous, St. Jacques increasingly annoyed, and Reginald Brock increasingly amused at the whole situation.

That morning, Barth had sat for a long hour, staring thoughtfully at the yellow-striped paper of his room, while he pondered the entire case. One by one, he passed over the events of the past six weeks in detailed review. He recalled those first days in Quebec, when his one idea had been to avoid the unsought society of the whole cordial American tribe. He bethought himself contentedly of his first aversion for Adolphe St. Jacques, which had been coördinate, in point of time, with his introduction to the dining-room of The Maple Leaf. He remembered the sunshiny morning which, following on the heels of a week of drizzle, had lured him forth to Sainte Anne-de-Beaupré and to his ultimate destruction.

Up to that time, his memories were orderly and logical. From that point onward, they fell into chaos. Days of grinding pain and intense dreariness were lightened by the sound of Nancy's low voice and the touch of Nancy's firm, supple fingers upon his injured foot. True, she had been an American; but, even at that early stage of his experience, it had begun to dawn upon Mr. Cecil Barth that, under proper conditions and in their proper places, Americans might have certain pleasing attributes. Then Nancy had left him. In the lonely days which followed, Barth had acknowledged to himself that, for Americans of a proper type, the proper conditions and the proper places bore direct connection with his own individual bottle of liniment. The acknowledgment was reached in the midst of his own efforts to establish relations with his own ankle which, all at once, seemed to him peculiarly remote and elusive. And then? Then he had returned to The Maple Leaf, and had found Nancy there, and she was the same Nancy, and there was a very jolly little tea shop in Saint Louis Street. At that point in his musings, Mr. Cecil Barth had seized his cap and rushed down the stairs of his ducal home.

Only once, as he was crossing through the Ring, did it occur to his mind, as a possible factor in the case, that, though a younger son, his departure for America had been attended by the wailing of a large chorus of mothers. Even then, he dismissed the thought as unworthy of Nancy and of himself. Details of that kind entered into the present situation not at all.

Fate was all in his favor, that morning. He found Nancy quite alone, and, as a result of his finding her, Nancy had been confronted by the tea-tray and the Britisher in combination.

"I don't see what you are laughing at," she said plaintively, in answer to Barth's merriment. "I am only trying to make my meaning unmistakable to you."

Barth laughed again.

"Oh, in time you would make a fairly good Englishwoman," he said reassuringly.

Only Nancy's super-acute ear could have discovered the note of condescension in his voice. She set down her teacup with a thump.

"Thank you; but I have no aspirations in that direction," she responded shortly.

"How strange!" Barth observed, as he took another scone, opened it and peered in to see which was the more buttery side.

"I don't see anything strange at all," Nancy argued. "Who wants to be English?"

Barth shut up the scone like a box, and laid it down on the edge of his saucer.

"I do."

"Well, you are. You ought to be satisfied."

In hot haste, Barth felt about for his glasses; but they were tangled in his buttons, and he missed them.

"Oh, rather!" he assented hurriedly. "Do have another scone."

Notwithstanding her indignation, Nancy laughed. Barth's accent was so like that of an elderly uncle bribing a naughty child to goodness by means of a stick of candy.

"Thank you, I always like hot biscuits," she assented. Then, for the second time, she put her elbows on the table and sat resting her chin upon her clasped hands. "Mr. Barth," she said meditatively; "has it ever occurred to you that I may possibly be proud of having been born an American?"

Barth peered up at her in near-sighted curiosity.

"Oh, no," he answered.

Nancy's eyes were fixed thoughtfully upon him, taking in every detail of his earnest face, honest and boyish, and likable withal.

"Well," she reiterated slowly; "I am."

"And you wouldn't rather be English, if you could?" Barth queried, with an eagerness for which she was at a loss to account.

"No. Why should I?"

He sat looking steadily at her, while the scarlet color mounted across his cheeks and brow. Then even Nancy's ears could not fail to distinguish the minor cadence in his voice, as he said, in slow regret,—

"I—I am sorry. I really can't see why."

CHAPTER EIGHTEEN

"And still," Dr. Howard added cheerily; "I wouldn't give up hope yet."

Adolphe St. Jacques turned from a listless contemplation of the habitant in the courtyard, and looked the doctor full in the face.

"You think—?" he said interrogatively.

The doctor's nod was plainly reluctant.

"Yes; but I do not know. It is impossible to tell. If I were in your place, I would hold on as long as I could, on the chance. Meanwhile, take things as easily as you can, and don't worry."

"It is sometimes harder to take things easily than to—"

St. Jacques was interrupted by a knock at the door, followed by a call from Nancy.

"May I come in, daddy?"

Hastily the young Frenchman turned to the doctor.

"And you won't speak to her about it yet?" he urged.

"No. I promise you to wait until you give me permission."

"Thank you," St. Jacques answered. "It is better to keep silent for the present. Still, it is a relief to have told you, and to know your opinion."

"Oh, daddy, I'm coming. I want to talk to you," Nancy reiterated.

Noiselessly the doctor slid back the bolt on the panelled door, just as Nancy turned the knob. It was done so deftly that the girl pushed open the door and entered the room, without in the least suspecting that she had walked in upon a secret conference.

"You here?" she said, nodding gayly to St. Jacques.

"Yes; but I am just going away."

"Don't hurry. I only came to ask my father a question or two. How much longer are we going to stay here, daddy?"

The doctor pressed together, tip to tip, the fingers of his two hands.

"I am sorry, Nancy," he answered a little deprecatingly; "but I am afraid it will take me fully three weeks longer to finish my work."

Her face fell.

"Is that all?"

"But I thought you were in a hurry to get home."

"I was; but I'm not," she answered, in terse contradiction.

St. Jacques laughed, as he bowed in exaggerated gratitude.

"Canada thanks you for the compliment, Miss Howard."

"It's not so much Canada as Quebec, not so much Quebec as it is The Maple Leaf," she replied. "It is going to be a great wrench, when I tear myself out of this place. But it will be three weeks at least, daddy?"

"Fully that."

Nancy twisted the letter in her hand.

"I've heard again from Joe, and he wants to come, the last of the week," she said slowly.

St. Jacques caught the note of discontent in her voice and smiled. It escaped the doctor, however, and he made haste to answer,—

"But we are always glad to see Joe. How long will he stay?"

"Two or three days. He has never been here, and he expects me to show him the sights of Quebec. Imagine me, M. St. Jacques, doing the tourist patter, as I take him the grand round!" Then she turned back to her father. "Joe obviously has something on his mind, daddy. You don't suppose it is a case of Persis Routh."

The doctor laughed.

"Jealous, Nancy?"

"Of course I am. Joe is my especial property, you know. Besides, I don't like Persis."

The doctor laughed again.

"Neither do I. Still, she is wonderfully pretty."

"Yes," Nancy added disconsolately; "and she doesn't have red hair and a consequent pain in her temper. Daddy?"

"Yes." With his back to the two young people, the doctor was cramming some papers into his limp portfolio.

"Were you going to walk with me, this afternoon?"

"No, my dear; I wasn't."

"But you promised."

"When?"

"At dinner, yesterday. You promised that, if I would let you off then, you would go with me, to-day."

"Did I? I am sorry. Really, Nancy, I can't go."

"But it is a perfect day."

"I don't doubt it; but I have an appointment with the ghost of Monseigneur Laval. Both his time and mine are precious."

"But I want to go," Nancy said, with a suspicion of a pout.

"Where?"

"Out to Sillery."

The doctor looked at her in benign rebuke.

"Nancy, it is eight miles to Sillery and back, and your father is short of wind. Even if Monseigneur Laval's ghost were not calling me, I couldn't be tempted to take any such tramp as that."

Just then, though apparently by chance, St. Jacques stepped forward. The doctor's eyes lighted, as they fell upon this possible substitute.

"You'd better ask M. St. Jacques to go, Nancy. I was just advising him to be out in the open air as much as possible."

Nancy's spine stiffened slightly, but quite perceptibly. Much as she liked St. Jacques and enjoyed his society, it was no part of her plan to accept his escort, when it was offered by a third person.

"M. St. Jacques has lectures and things to go to, daddy," she said, with an accent of calm rebuke.

St. Jacques started to speak; but the doctor forestalled him.

"Then he'd better cut the lectures. There may be such a thing as working too hard."

Nancy felt a swift longing to administer personal chastisement to her father. She wondered if good men were, of their very goodness, bound to be unduly guileless. She bit her lip. Then she smiled sweetly at St. Jacques.

"But M. St. Jacques may have other plans for the afternoon."

This time, the Frenchman took the matter into his own hands.

"As soon as it becomes my turn to speak—" he interpolated.

"Well?" Nancy inquired obdurately.

"I should like to say that I have nothing to do, this afternoon; that I was wishing for a walk, and that no other comrade would be half so enjoyable as Miss Nancy Howard."

"Oh," Nancy responded. "Is that all?"

"It is enough. Will you go?"

She hesitated.

"If my father hasn't decoyed you into the trap, quite against your will."

St. Jacques raised his brows.

"Did you ever know me to say things for the mere sake of being polite?"

"No," Nancy said honestly; "I never did."

"Then where is your hat?"

Nancy laughed. Then she departed to wrestle with her hat pins, while the good doctor rubbed his hands with pleasure over the successful tact with which he had won his uninterrupted afternoon.

A round hour later, they stood on the church steps, looking down upon Sillery Cove. One starlit night, long years before, a young general, indomitable in the presence of mortal disease as in the face of an impregnable foe, had dropped down the river to land at that spot and, scaling the cliff, to fight his way to his victorious death. Now the dropping tide had left a broad beach, and the Cove lay in heavy shadow; but, beyond, the open stream flashed blue in the sunlight. Full to the northward, the windows in the rifle factory caught the light and tossed it back to them, dazzling as the glory which Wolfe, landing in the Cove, was fated to find awaiting him upon those selfsame Plains. Still farther beyond, the rock city lay, a gray mound against the vivid blue of the distant hills, and above its crest, even from afar, Nancy could distinguish the blood-red dot which flutters each day from dawn to dusk above the cannon on the King's Bastion.

"Do you care to see the inside of the church?" St. Jacques asked her.

"Of course. I may never come here again, and I am growing to love your churches," Nancy answered, suddenly calling herself back from a dream of the day when the golden lilies floated above the Citadel, and of the night when the fleet of English boats crept noiselessly up the river to face—and win—a forlorn hope of victory. Then abruptly she faced St. Jacques. "Bigot or no Bigot, right or wrong, my sympathies are sometimes with the French," she said. "Wolfe was a hero; but I can't help siding with the under dog, even if he is coated with gold and fat with bones."

St. Jacques smiled at her outburst.

"And the under dog is always grateful," he replied briefly. "Come!"

Cap in hand, he led the way into the empty church, made his swift genuflection before the altar, and turned to look at Nancy. The girl stood a step or two in the rear, glancing about her at the arching roof and at the decorations of the chancel. St. Jacques hesitated.

"If Mademoiselle will excuse me," he said then, for the first time in their acquaintance speaking in his native tongue. And, without waiting for Nancy to reply, he went swiftly forward, bowed for a moment at the altar rail, then turned and knelt before the first of the painted Stations of the Cross.

It was done with the simple unconsciousness of a child to whom his religion was a matter of every-day experience. Nevertheless, as Nancy stepped noiselessly into a pew and rested her cheek on her clasped fingers, she knew by instinct that her companion was in no normal mood. It was not for nothing that Nancy had watched the sturdy little Frenchman during the past month. Watching him now, she could see the pallor underneath his swarthiness, see the sudden weakening of his resolute chin, and the pitiful curve of the thin lips. Then, all at once, St. Jacques covered his face with his slim, dark hands, and Nancy could see nothing more. Involuntarily she wondered whether she might not already have seen too much.

St. Jacques was smiling, when he joined her at the door; but they both were rather silent, as they went down the interminable flight of steps which leads to Champlain Street, and came out on the broad beach of sand that borders the Cove when the tide is low. Even during their brief delay in the church, the short afternoon had waned perceptibly, and the sun had dropped beneath the crest of the point. Behind their backs, the bluff rose in a wall of deep purple rock, at their right it was splashed with an occasional dot of color where some sheltered maple still held its crown of ruddy leaves. The river beside them flowed on noiselessly, swiftly, relentlessly as time itself, in a level sheet of steely gray. But, beyond the gray, relentless flowing, there rose the stately cliffs of Lévis, solid, permanent and bathed in a glow of mingled purple and gold.

As they rounded the Cove with its rotting, moss-grown piers, and reached the point whence Champlain Street runs in a straight-cut line at the base of the cliff, St. Jacques came out of his silence, and began to talk once more. At first, Nancy stared at him in amazement. In all their acquaintance, she had seen him in no such mood of rattling gayety. The words flew from his tongue, now English, now French, framing themselves into every conceivable sort of quip and whim and jest. He laughed at Nancy for her lusty Americanism, predicted her conversion to Canadian life and ways, made sport of his own experiences when he had come, a stranger, to Laval and Quebec. He laughed about Barth and eulogized him by turns, paused to give a word of hearty admiration to Brock, and then rushed on into a merry account of his boyhood among the little brothers and sisters in the quiet French home at Rimouski. Then, as they mounted the little rise beneath Cape Diamond, his merriment fell from him like the falling of a mask.

"Miss Howard," he said suddenly; "do you remember the sword of Damocles?"

"Yes," she assented, at a loss for the key to this new mood. "What of it?"

He pointed up to the cliff.

"That. They were all at supper, resting and happy after the day, playing with their little children, perhaps, when the rock fell upon them. There was no warning, and there were tons and tons of the rock. Seventy-eight were found, and their coffins were placed together in one huge pile before the altar rails. Nobody knows how many more are buried under this little hill in the road. It was impossible to move away the stone; they could only level it as best they could, and build above it a road for the living to walk on."

Nancy shivered. All at once she became aware of the chill that swept in from the river, of the growing dusk which the scattered electric lights were powerless to break. Above her, the cliff towered in sinister, threatening dignity; and the houses below leaned to its face impotently, as if their weakness appealed to its strength for mercy and support.

St. Jacques drew a deep breath.

"It is no easy thing to live on steadily under an overhanging fate," he said, half to himself.

But Nancy heard and wondered.

Then, from the heart of the dusk far up the river, there came a distant throbbing. It grew nearer, more distinct, until they could make out the dim outline of a mighty ocean-going steamer. In steady majesty it swept down upon them, glowing with lights from stem to stern, passed them by and, only a few hundred feet beyond them, paused to drift idly on the current, as it sent out its shrill call for a pilot.

The sudden whistle roused St. Jacques from his absorption. He shook himself free from his mood, and faced Nancy again with a laughing face.

"Come," he said. "Supper is calling, and we must hurry."

Merrily they picked their way along the darkening tunnel of Little Champlain Street, merrily they slid upward in the dismal wooden recesses of the elevator, merrily they tramped along Sainte Anne Street and halted at the door of The Maple Leaf.

On the threshold, Nancy faced St. Jacques with merry eyes.

"Thank you so much for my glorious walk," she said eagerly. "Confess that it has been a most jovial occasion."

But all the merriment had fled from the dark eyes of St. Jacques.

"Perhaps," he assented gravely. "But a true Frenchman often smiles most gayly when he has been hardest hit." And, cap in hand, he stood aside to let Nancy pass in before him.

CHAPTER NINETEEN

International complications had arisen at the supper table. Confronted by an English menu, the four elderly Frenchmen had held a hasty consultation over a new item which had appeared thereon. Their minds were strictly logical; they had come to the conclusion that sweetbreads were a species of cake, and they had ordered accordingly.

"*Mais oui*," one of them observed, as he gravely prodded the resultant tidbit with his knife and fork. "Vat ees eet?"

"Them's the sweetbreads," responded the waitress, who was an Hibernian and scanty of grammar.

There followed an anxious pause, while four prodding forks worked in unison.

"*Huitres?*" suggested one Frenchman.

"*Côtelettes?*" added the second.

"*C'est bon*," said the third, more daring than his companions.

But the fourth pushed aside his plate.

"*C'est dommage!*" he exclaimed, and Nancy, who shared his opinion, took refuge in her napkin.

She emerged to find Brock just taking his place beside her, and she looked up with a welcoming smile. After the too obvious devotion of the Englishman, after the self-repressed, high-strung temperament of St. Jacques, Nancy was always conscious of a certain sense of relief in the society of the jovial Canadian. It is no slight gift to be always merry, always thoughtful of the comfort of one's companions, always at peace with one's self and with the world. This gift Brock possessed in its entirety. Without him at her elbow, Nancy would have passed many a lonely hour in Quebec. An own brother could not have been more undemonstratively careful to heed her slightest wish. Best of all, Brock had a trick of placing himself at her service, not at all as if he were in love with her; but merely as if it were the one thing possible for him to do.

Just once, their friendship had lacked little of coming to grief. On the evening after the market episode, Nancy had gathered together her courage and had read Brock a long lecture upon his sins. An hour later, she had retired from the contest, worsted. With imperturbable good nature, Brock had assented to her charges against him. Then, swiftly turning the tables, he had summed up all of Barth's vulnerable points and had accused her of increasing their number by an injudicious system of coddling. Nancy's hair was red, her temper by no means imperturbable. She had defended herself with vigor and clearness. Then, with snapping eyes, she had stalked away out of the room, leaving Brock, serene and smiling, in undisturbed possession of the field. The next morning, Brock had been called out of town on business. When he returned, two days later, Nancy had met him with whole-hearted smiles. Without Brock's genial presence, the atmosphere of The Maple Leaf became altogether too fully charged with electricity for her liking. From that time onward, Nancy remembered her hair, and fought shy of argument with the tall Canadian whose very imperturbability only rendered him the more maddening foe.

"You look as if you had heard some good news," she assured him, even while he was unfolding his napkin.

Brock smiled with conscious satisfaction.

"So I have."

"Tell me."

"Not now."

"How long must I wait?"

"A week."

"How unkind of you, when you know I am consumed with curiosity!"

With the butterknife in his hand, Brock turned. Nancy, as she looked far into the depths of those clear gray eyes of his, was suddenly aware that all was right with Brock's world. Moreover, she was aware that he was as eager as she herself for the week to pass away and give him the chance to speak.

"Then I really must wait," she assented to the look in his eyes. "A week is a long time. Meanwhile, I have some news."

"Good, I hope."

"Certainly. We are expecting a guest, next Friday."

"How unlucky for him!" Brock observed.

"Are you superstitious?"

"No; but you are."

She raised her brows in question, and Brock answered the unspoken words.

"Otherwise, why do you carry a pocket edition of Sainte Anne-de-Beaupré?"

"How do you know I do?"

"Because it fell out on the floor just now, when I upset your coat. It is a very superior little Sainte Anne, made of silver."

This time, Nancy had the grace to blush. Only the day before, she had come into possession of the dainty toy.

"That's not superstition," she answered; "it is merely an effigy of my patron saint."

Brock nodded.

"For the name? I suspect I could tell who chose it."

Again Nancy's brows rose inquiringly.

"If you like," she said composedly.

"Barth, of course."

"No. I knew you would say so. Now you have forfeited your one guess," she responded smilingly, yet with an odd little tugging at her heart, as she recalled the face of St. Jacques, as he had laid the little silver image into her outstretched palm.

"Make her your patron saint as well," he had said briefly. "The time may come when I shall need the prayers of her name-child to help me at her shrine."

And Nancy, looking straight into his dark eyes, had given the promise that he asked.

But now, with full intention, she was seeking to drive St. Jacques from her mind.

"You don't ask about our guest," she added.

"No." Brock buttered his bread with calm deliberation. "I knew you would tell me, when you were ready."

She fell into the trap laid by his apparent indifference.

"I am ready now. It is an old friend of ours from New York, Mr. Joseph Churchill."

"So glad he is an old friend," Brock responded coolly.

"Why?"

"Because he won't complicate things, as a young man would do."

"Mr. Churchill is twenty-five," Nancy remarked a little severely.

"We call that rather young up here. Will he stop long?"

"A day or two."

Brock helped himself to marmalade.

"And he comes, next Friday?"

"Yes."

"Right, oh! See that he gets out of the way by Monday. The Maple Leaf is quite full enough, as it is."

"But he is going to the Chateau," Nancy explained.

"Lucky fellow to have money enough! In his place, I should probably have to seek the Lower Town. What are you going to do with him?"

Nancy smiled ingratiatingly.

"Just what I was meaning to ask you, Mr. Brock."

Brock's answering laugh sent Barth's fingers in search of the string of his eyeglasses.

"There's a snug little cell empty up at the Citadel," he suggested. "Take him up there and let him see how he likes military hospitality. He could put in a very instructive two days, studying the position of the Bunker Hill cannon."

Two days later, Nancy stood in the extreme bow of the Lévis ferry. Beside her, blond and big and altogether bonny, stood Mr. Joseph Churchill, obviously an American, equally obviously from New York. At the stern, in the lee of the deck house, Dr. Howard was doing his best to shelter himself from the cutting wind.

Nancy and the New Yorker were in full tide of conversation. No hint of regret had marked Nancy's manner, as she had stood scanning the doors of the sleeping-cars. Before Lévis was a river-breadth behind, she had gathered from her companion a detailed account of the early gayeties of the season, had filled his ears with the more sober charms of quaint Quebec, and had drawn a vivid outline of the more salient characteristics of Mr. Reginald Brock. Of Barth and St. Jacques, she had omitted to make any mention.

Upon one point, the doctor was rigid. Churchill might register at the Chateau, if he insisted. He must take his meals with them at The Maple Leaf. And so it came about that Barth's first intimation that a guest was expected, occurred when he looked up from his tea, that night, to greet Nancy as she came into the room, and discovered the huge, sleek American at Nancy's side.

"Oh, by George!" remarked Mr. Cecil Barth, and promptly dropped his bread, butter-side down, into the starched recesses of his immaculate white waistcoat.

Later, he sought the parlor. Over his shoulder, he had heard the gay voices of Brock and Nancy, and the deeper chest tones of the burly American. He felt an acute longing to put on his glasses and, screwing himself about in his chair, to take a prolonged stare at the intruder. His hurried glance had given him the impression of vast stature combined with the workmanship of an unexceptionable tailor. But where did the fellow come from? What was the fellow doing there? And what, oh, by George, what was the fellow's connection with Nancy?

"I'd like to punch him," Mr. Cecil Barth muttered vengefully to himself. "Oh, rather!"

He found the parlor quite deserted. St. Jacques, who had met Churchill earlier in the afternoon, had betaken himself to his room. Brock and the Howards, with their guest, were still at the table. Accordingly, Barth pulled a book from his pocket and sat himself down to wait. He waited long. When at last Nancy led the way into the parlor, Barth was surprised to miss Brock from her train. Under such conditions, it was inconceivable to him that the Canadian should not have stood his ground. The parlor was common property. He himself would sit there forever, rather than let himself be ousted by any American, least of all an American who would bedeck himself with jewelry as uncouth as the hymnbook of blue and gold that dangled from this American's fob. Barth had always heard that Americans were stiffed-necked dissenters. Nevertheless, he had never supposed they would find it needful to advertise their dissent by means of enamelled trinkets. He wrapped himself in his Britishism, and sat tight in his chair, waiting to see what would occur.

Nothing occurred. Nancy gave him her usual friendly smile and nod. Then, crossing the room, she settled herself on a sofa and, making room for Churchill at her side, dropped into animated talk of places and persons who were totally remote from Barth's previous knowledge. Now and then, she glanced across at him carelessly. Now and then, her huge companion turned and bestowed upon him a rebuking stare which said, plainly as words could have done, that his further presence there was needless.

Regardless of the fact that he knew Nancy was fully aware he never read through his glasses, Barth remained stolidly on guard, glasses on nose and nose apparently in his book. Now and then, however, he lowered his book and refreshed himself with a smile at Nancy, or a scowl at the unconscious back of Nancy's companion.

At length, Nancy could endure the situation no longer. Much as she liked Barth, she could willingly have dispensed with his society, just then. After their weeks of separation, she and Churchill had much to talk over, and she found the presence of an outsider a check upon the freedom of their dialogue. So sure had she been of Barth's prompt and tactful withdrawal that she had made no effort to introduce him, when they had first entered the room. Her plans for the next day were formed to include the young Englishman. For that one evening, she had intended to give her attention entirely to her guest. Now, however, she saw that an introduction was fast becoming a matter of social necessity, and she tried to prepare the way for it.

During the space of a minute, she permitted the talk with Churchill to lapse. Then, meeting Barth's eyes above the deckled edges of his book, she smiled across at him in the friendly, informal fashion he had learned to know and to like so well.

"I thought you were bound for the theatre, this evening, Mr. Barth," she said.

It was a wholly random bullet; but it met its billet. Barth reddened. In his interest in Nancy's companion, he had entirely forgotten his explicit announcement of his evening's plan.

"Oh, no," he answered nonchalantly.

"Then men do occasionally change their minds. Isn't it a good play?"

"Oh, yes," he answered again, still more nonchalantly.

Turning slightly, Churchill looked across at the slender, boyish figure at the farther side of the room. His glance was disrespectful, and Barth was keenly conscious of the disrespect. He made a manful effort to assert himself.

"Jolly sort of night, Miss Howard," was the only bubble that effervesced from his mind.

Nancy felt a wave of petulant sympathy sweeping over her. Long experience of her guest had taught her the meaning of that swift motion of his head and shoulders, and she feared what might follow, both for Barth's sake and her own. She dreaded any possible injury to the feelings of the young Englishman; she dreaded still more the hearing Churchill's irreverent comments upon a man whom she had grown proud to number among her loyal friends. Never had Barth appeared more impenetrably dull, never more obdurately British! It was the mockery of fate. Just when she was praying that he might be at his best, he turned monosyllabic, and then completed his disgrace by talking about the weather. Meanwhile her annoyance was forcing all ideas from her own brain, and her answering question was equally banal.

"Is it cold, to-night?"

Barth was not impenetrable, by any means. He felt Nancy's embarrassment, was keenly alive to her efforts in his behalf. The knowledge only rendered him more tongue-tied than ever; but his blue eyes smiled eagerly back at her, as he responded, with admirable brevity,—

"Oh, rather!"

"Joe, what is it?" Nancy demanded, as she followed her strangling guest out into the hall.

Churchill was walking to and fro, coughing and teary.

"Nancy Howard," he said, as soon as he could speak; "will you kindly tell me what manner of thing that is?"

Then Nancy asserted herself. Erect and gracious in her dainty evening gown, she turned back and stood on the threshold.

"Mr. Barth," she said, in a quiet tone of command; "will you please come here and be introduced to my cousin? Mr. Churchill, I want you to meet my friend," an almost imperceptible pause added emphasis to the word; "my friend, Mr. Cecil Barth."

CHAPTER TWENTY

"And this," the guide continued, with the loquacity of his kind; "directly at our feet is the River Saint Lawrence. That building there with the pointed roofs is the Chateau Frontenac, built on the exact site of the old Chateau de Saint Louis. Beyond it, you see the spire of the French Basilica, consecrated in sixteen hundred and sixty-six, and, slightly to the right, are the roofs and spires of Laval."

"And, right under our noses, the city of Quebec, huddled indiscriminately around The Maple Leaf," Brock interrupted, as their red-coated escort stopped for breath. "Miss Howard, I wish you hadn't been quite so generous in your fee."

"But I am sure it is very interesting," Churchill observed politely. "Remember that I am a stranger here."

The guide took the hint and edged towards Churchill's end of the line.

"This is what is termed the King's Bastion," he went on glibly. "Beyond is Cape Diamond, so called from the crystals of quartz that used to be found there. Now they are very rare; but," with every appearance of anxiety, he fell to searching his pockets; "but I happen to have—"

Again Brock interrupted.

"No use, Thomas Atkins," he said jovially. "We are too old birds to be caught in that trap."

Unabashed, the guide let the bits of quartz drop back into his pocket.

"Many ladies admire my buttons," he said tentatively. "They make interesting hat pins."

"The ladies, or the buttons?" Nancy queried innocently. "But, thank you, I think you have showed us everything, and we can find our way out alone." And, leaving the bastion, she led the way back to the tiny cannon of Bunker Hill, where she loyally halted her companions.

A cloudless sky arched above the old gray Citadel, that morning. Inside the walls, the daily routine was going its usual leisurely course. Few visitors were abroad; but an occasional private strayed across the enclosure and, not far from the gate, guard-mounting was just taking place. Nancy watched the new guard as it tramped out into the open, saluted and went into position, its every evolution followed in detail by the stout Newfoundland dog who waddled along at its heels. Then, as the band swung about and marched off for its daily practice, she moved away.

"Come," she said a little impatiently. "After the glorious past, the present is a bit of anticlimax. Shall we go for a walk?"

Her companions assented, and together they went down into Saint Louis Street and turned towards the terrace. As they passed Barth's quarters, he unexpectedly appeared upon the steps.

"Whither?" Nancy called blithely, as he lifted his cap.

"To post some letters."

"Come with us, instead," she bade him, notwithstanding the murmured protestations which arose from both Brock and Churchill.

To Nancy's mind, the previous evening had not been altogether a shining success. For half an hour after their introduction, she had dragged the two men through a species of conversation; but there had been a triple sigh of relief as the evening gun had marked the hour for Barth's departure. Nancy had followed him to the parlor door.

"Good night," she said cordially there. "We shall see you, in the morning?"

"Oh,—yes. If I can," Barth answered vaguely.

Then he had made a dejected exit. As he strolled languidly away to his room, he alternated between fears of a possible relapse in his ankle, and mutinous thoughts regarding the hero of Valley Forge.

"Beastly race, those American men!" was the finale of his reflections. "Oh, rather!"

Now, however, his dejection vanished in the face of the sunshiny morning and of Nancy's greeting.

"Won't I be in the way?" he asked.

"Why should you?"

"I can't walk much, you know."

"But I thought Englishmen were famous for their walking," Churchill said, as he greeted the young Englishman much as a genial mastiff might salute a youthful pug.

Barth glanced towards Nancy with a confident smile.

"Didn't Miss Howard tell you?" he asked.

"Tell me what?"

"About the way we first met. I sprained my ankle, and Miss Howard turned into a hired nurse, and took care of me."

Churchill's eyes sought Nancy's scarlet face.

"The deuce she did! Where was this party?"

"This—?"

"This party?"

"Oh, no. It wasn't a party at all. I was entirely by myself. I have sometimes wondered how she ever chanced to find me in all that crowd."

"Probably the Good Sainte Anne guided her unworthy namesake," Nancy responded lightly. "That was where the tragedy occurred."

"Oh!" Beside Barth's *oh*, that of Churchill seemed needlessly crisp and curt. "But I thought you were bored to death at Sainte Anne-de-Beaupré, Nancy."

"That was only at first. Later, events happened."

"So I should judge. Strange you forgot to mention them!"

"There are unexplained gaps in your own letters," she reminded him audaciously. "It was only by chance that I heard whom you took out, the night of the Leighton dinner." Then she turned to the others. "We mustn't go far, this morning," she added; "not so much on account of your foot, Mr. Barth, as because of our early dinner. Shall we take ourselves to the terrace?"

High up on the glacis in the lee of the King's Bastion, they found a belated bit of Indian summer. Nancy dropped down on the crisp, dry turf and, turning, beckoned St. Jacques to her side. Crossing the terrace with Barth, she had seen the Frenchman pacing to and fro beside the rail, and she had answered his wishful greeting with a smile of welcome. Leaving Brock and Churchill to lead the way, Nancy had sauntered idly along in the rear, adjusting her quick step to the frailties of Barth's ankle, her alert happiness to the darker mood which sat heavily upon her other companion.

"You are not going to fail us, this afternoon, M. St. Jacques?" she asked now.

Silently he shook his head.

"Your cousin has a perfect day," he said, after a pause.

"And he appreciates it. Already, he declares himself the slave of the place."

"You are coming with me, in the morning?" St. Jacques inquired.

"I am not sure. I hope we can; but Mr. Churchill is not a very good Catholic," she answered, with a smile.

St. Jacques's eyes lighted mirthfully.

"But Sainte Anne is his patron saint?" he questioned.

Nancy shook her head.

"Alas, no! He has shifted his allegiance, and poor Sainte Anne is feeling very much cut up about it."

"No matter," St. Jacques answered philosophically. "She is getting her fair share of devotees, and, with France and England at her shrine, she can afford to be content without America." Then his face darkened. "If only she will be propitious!" he added, with sudden gravity.

Nancy's hand shut on a tuft of grass at her side. Slowly she had come, during those past days, to the realization of the dual personality of the patron saint of Adolphe St. Jacques. Half human, half divine, the Good Sainte Anne was holding complete sway in the mind of the young Frenchman, just then. Half his unspoken wish was plain to her, half was still beyond her ken. She wondered restlessly when would come the time that she was free to speak. She wondered, too, what were the words she was destined to say.

With a swift motion, St. Jacques settled backward to rest his elbow on the grass at her side. Pushing back his cap, as if its slight weight irritated him, he swept the dark hair from his forehead. Nancy frowned involuntarily as her eyes rested on the angry scar.

"That was a shocking blow," she said pityingly.

He nodded, with slow thoughtfulness. Then he bit his lip, and shook his hair forward until the scar was completely hidden.

"It might have been worse—perhaps."

"You'd better ask the Good Sainte Anne to do a miracle on you," Brock suggested, from his place farther up the slope.

Instantly the dark eyes sought Nancy's face.

"I have already asked her," Adolphe St. Jacques answered quietly.

"And what did the lady say?"

The Frenchman's eyes moved northward and rested upon the purple tops of the far-off Laurentides.

"My novena is not finished. She has yet to make her answer," he said.

And, for the second time in their acquaintance, Nancy was conscious of the dull tugging at her heart. Forgetful of Barth, watching from the other side, she turned to look straight down into the face of St. Jacques; and Brock, who alone of them all had been taken into the heart of the Frenchman's secret, felt it no shame to himself when the tears rushed into his clear gray eyes, as he saw the look on Nancy's face, womanly, earnest, yet all unconscious of impending ill.

It was Churchill who broke the silence. A stranger to them all but Nancy, he yet could not fail to realize the tension of the moment. Nevertheless he assured himself that he had met those symptoms before. Nancy's path, the past season, had been strewn with similar victims.

"Wonderful view!" he said calmly.

The platitude broke the strain. St. Jacques sat up and put on his cap, and Barth fumbled for his glasses. Above them, Brock openly rubbed his eyes with the bunched-up fingers of his gloves.

"So glad you like it, Joe! It is wonderful; and then it is endeared to me by all manner of associations. Away up there in those blue hills, Mr. Barth sprained his ankle; M. St. Jacques and I spent an afternoon in this road just underneath the cliff, and," her eyes sought Brock's eyes mockingly; "and there aren't ten blocks in the entire city that can't mark some sort of a skirmish between the American and Canadian forces."

Brock's answering shot was prompt.

"It is only that America refuses to be annexed," he supplemented gravely. "We hope to bring her to terms in time."

And Barth fell to kicking the turf in moody discontent. Nancy checked him.

"Don't destroy the glacis of your chief American outpost, Mr. Barth. You may need it sometime to fight off the French from your possessions."

Her words had been wholly free from any allegorical meaning. Nevertheless, Barth's heels ground into the turf more viciously than ever, as he made grim answer,—

"Oh, we English need no artificial defenses to fight off the Frenchmen, you know."

"Sic 'em!" Brock observed impartially. Then he snatched his hat from his head, and, forgetful of their differences, Barth and St. Jacques followed his lead.

Distant and faint from behind the sheltering wall came the strains of *God Save the King*, as the band marched back from practice.

"Strange to hear *America* up here!" Churchill said idly.

"*America?*" The Frenchman's accent was inquiring.

"Yes. That is our national anthem."

"How long since?" Brock queried coolly.

"Why, always, I suppose."

Barth bestowed a contemplative stare upon the stranger.

"How very—American!" he observed.

"Of course. We think it is rather characteristic, and are no end proud of it," Churchill assured him blandly.

Barth sat up, straight and stiff.

"Mr. Churchill, did you ever happen to hear of *God Save the King?*"

"Queen? Oh, beg pardon! She's dead, and it is a king now. Yes, I've heard of it. What about it?"

"That." Barth swept his little gray cap towards the dying notes of the final phrase. "Your so-called *America* is only our *God Save the King*."

"Is it? I'm no musician, and didn't know. Still, I can't see that it hurts it, to have started with you. So did we all, if it comes to that."

"Then you should give us the credit for having originated it," Brock suggested.

St. Jacques rolled over on his other elbow.

"As it happens, Brock, you didn't originate it. It came from the other side of the Channel."

"Oh, rather! But it's ours," Barth interposed hastily.

St. Jacques rolled back again.

"I beg your pardon, Mr. Barth; but it chances to be French," he returned quietly. "Lulli wrote it for Louis Quatorze, and England borrowed it without returning thanks." And then, still leaning on his elbow with his eyes fixed upon Barth, he sang to the end the good old song,—

"Grand Dieu! Sauvez le Roi!

Grand Dieu! Sauvez le Roi!

Sauvez le Roi!

Que toujours glorieux,

Louis Victorieux,

Voye ses ennemis

Toujours soumis."

As the light baritone voice died on the still air, Nancy looked down at him with a smile.

"France scores, this time," she said. "But what a text for an international alliance! Here we are, three nations sitting under the eaves of the most famous citadel in America, and each claiming as his very own the same national anthem."

"Oh; but it is generally admitted to belong to us," Barth added, with unflinching persistence.

The next night, Churchill and the doctor were left alone for a few moments. The doctor held out his hand with a smile.

"Nancy tells me you are open to congratulation, Joe."

"Yes. That is what brought me up here. I am too fond of you both to be willing to take your congratulations in ink. She is a wonderful girl, Uncle Ross." The happiness of the young American sat well upon him. In his uncle's eyes, he gained dignity, even as he spoke those few words. Then he laughed. "You may find yourself in the face of a similar situation," he suggested.

"What do you mean?"

"Nancy."

The doctor stared at him for a moment.

"Oh, not a bit! Not a bit!" he said then. "Every lover is looking for love. Nancy is nothing but a little girl."

Churchill smiled.

"Then look out for your little girl. You may lose her, some day."

"No," the doctor protested valiantly. "The Lady will see to that. They are nice boys, good boys; but they are only children."

"Don't be too sure. If I know anything at all about such matters—"

"You don't," the doctor interrupted testily. "But go on! Go on!"

"Then St. Jacques is very much in love with Nancy; and, what is more, that snip of an Englishman is in love with her, too."

"Hh! And what about Brock?" growled the doctor.

Churchill thrust his hands into his pockets and smiled back into the frowning face of his uncle.

"That's where you have me," he answered coolly. "I have been watching the two of them, all day long, and I'll be sanctified if I can tell you now."

CHAPTER TWENTY-ONE

Four days after Churchill took his departure from Quebec and its Maple Leaf, Brock came striding into the dining-room, his head erect, his gray eyes shining.

"Miss Howard, you are going for a walk, this afternoon," he said, as he drew back his chair.

"How do you know?"

"Because I am counting on you. Have you anything else to do?"

"I was going to the library," she suggested. "The new magazines are just in."

"Let them wait," he said coolly. "It is too fine a day to be wasted over a fire and a book. I'll not only show you a new picture; but I promise to tell you a better story than any that ever was written into a magazine."

Nancy looked up into his happy eyes.

"Then the week is over?" she questioned.

"At last."

She laughed at his accent of relief.

"How impatient you were! Your secret must have preyed upon you."

"Not so bad as that," he began; but she interrupted him mockingly.

"And how many people have you been telling, in the meantime?"

"Not one."

"Truthfully?"

"Yes. I wanted to tell you, first of all."

She smiled back at him fearlessly.

"Thank you. I appreciate it."

"And will you go?"

"Of course," she answered heartily. "Did a woman ever refuse to listen to a secret?"

An hour later, she joined him in the hall. Brock stared at her approvingly. Her dark green cloth gown was the work of a tailor of sorts; the plumes of her wide hat made an admirable setting for her halo of ruddy hair. And Nancy returned the approval in full measure. Few men were better to look upon than was Reginald Brock, tall and supple, his well-set head thatched with crisp brown hair and lighted with those merry, clear gray eyes. No sinister thought had ever left its line on Brock's honest, manly face.

"Come, then," he said, as he opened the door. "You are in my hands, this afternoon."

He led the way to the Lower Town. Then, leaving Notre Dame des Victoires far behind them, they passed the custom house, crossed to the Louise Embankment and, rounding the angle by the immigration sheds, came out on the end of the Commissioners' Wharf.

"There!" Brock said triumphantly. "What do you think of this?"

Nancy drew a long breath of sheer delight.

"One can't think; one can only feel," she said slowly.

The river, lying deep blue in the yellow sunlight, slid past their very feet, its glittering wavelets crossed and recrossed with silvery reflections caught from the sky above. Far down its course, the dark indigo Laurentides seemed jutting out into the stream that washed their feet. Above was the Citadel, a crown of gray upon its purplish cliff. Behind them, the noise of the city lost itself in the murmur of the hurrying tide. Close at hand, a network of cables was lowering freight into the hold of an ocean-going steamer; and, out in the middle of the stream, a clumsy craft, loaded to the water's edge, crawled sluggishly upward against current and tide, ready for the morrow's market.

Brock pointed to an unused anchor, close to the edge of the embankment.

"Shall we sit down?" he asked.

Nancy took her place in silence. Silently he dropped down beside her. It was a long time before the stillness was broken, save by the lapping of the river at their feet and the hoarse cries of the men in the steamer's hold. For the moment, they were as isolated as if they had been in some remote desert, rather than upon the edge of one of the busiest spots of the entire city.

Brock's impatience appeared to have left him. With his gaze on the river, he was whistling almost inaudibly to himself; but it was plain to Nancy, as she watched him, that his thoughts were altogether pleasant ones. So were her own, for the matter of that. The past month had been a happy one to her, and Brock had caused some of its happiest memories. She had trusted him completely, and she had never known him to fail her. His chivalry, his courtesy, his brother-like care had been for her, from the hour of their meeting. She could still recall the glad look in his eyes, as they had rested upon her when he entered the dining-room, that first night. From that hour onward, Nancy Howard and Reginald Brock had been sure, each of the other's friendship.

"What about it?" Brock asked, as he suddenly turned to face her.

"About what?"

"The subject of your thoughts."

"All good things," she answered unhesitatingly. "I was thinking about you, just then."

"And wishing me good?"

"All good, even as you have been good to me," she responded, with quiet dignity.

He smiled.

"Nothing to count. But now for the picture."

"It is beautiful beyond words."

He smiled again.

"Wait. You haven't seen it yet."

With a quick motion of his hand, he drew his watch from his pocket, opened the case and held it out to Nancy. There was no cloud of reservation in the girl's happy eyes, as she looked at the picture within.

"Mr. Brock!"

"Yes?"

His accent was full of happy question. Downright and prompt came Nancy's answer.

"She is adorable."

Gently he took the watch from her hand and looked steadily at the picture, a picture of a round girlish face set as proudly as Brock's own upon its shapely shoulders.

"Yes," he assented slowly. "Better than that, she is good."

There was no mistaking the gladness in Nancy's tone, as she responded,—

"I think I was never more delighted in all my life. You were good to tell me, first of all."

"I wanted to," Brock replied, with boyish eagerness. "We've been such good chums, all this last month, that I was sure you would be interested. I want you to meet her. We weren't going to announce it just yet; but I coaxed her to hurry it up a little, so I could bring her to call on you, before you go home."

Nancy still held the picture in her hand.

"Is she really as pretty as this?" she asked.

"Why,—yes, I suppose so. I used to think so. Lately, I haven't thought much about her looks, one way or the other," he confessed. "She always seems to me about right, and she knows things, too. Really, Miss Howard," as he spoke, he faced Nancy, with his eyes shining; "really, I'm in great luck. It isn't every day that a girl of her sort falls in love with a fellow like me."

There was no hint of coquetry in Nancy's manner. With a frankness his own sister might have shown, she held out her hand in token of congratulation.

"I am not so sure of that," she answered, with a smile.

Then the pause lengthened. Brock's thoughts were far afield; Nancy's were fixed upon the man at her side. In all sincerity, she did rejoice at his unexpected tidings. No sentimental regrets entered into her perfect content. Her friendship for Brock had been friendship pure and simple; on neither side had it ever been mingled with a thought of love. From chance playmates of an October holiday, they had grown into a loyal liking which was to outlast many a dividing year and mile. And Brock deserved all good things, even the love of this dainty bit of girlhood whose eyes smiled bravely back into her own.

"Tell me all about it," she said at last.

Brock roused himself from his reverie.

"There's not so much to tell. I've known her always; we've always been good friends, but, last summer at Cacouna, it was—different."

Nancy smiled at the pause which added explanatory force to the last word.

"And was it then?"

"No; not till two or three weeks ago. You see, it took me a good while to get to where I dared speak about it."

"And when—?"

Brock looked up suddenly.

"I don't dare think of that yet, Miss Howard," he answered a bit unsteadily. "The present is so perfect that I am afraid to tempt Fate by asking anything more of the future. For the present, I am like the river out there," he pointed to the shining stream before him; "just drifting along in the sunshine."

And the sunshine found an answering light in Nancy's eyes, as, accepting his offered hand, she slowly rose to her feet and turned her face towards home.

CHAPTER TWENTY-TWO

The clouds hung gray and low over the old gray city. From the river the wind swept in, raw and cutting, and the Laurentides lay in the purple haze which betokens a coming storm. The terrace was deserted; the fountain in the Ring had stopped playing, and narrow Sainte Anne Street was turned into a tunnel thick with flying dust. Indian summer was at an end, and winter was at hand.

With her ruddy hair flying and her broad hat tilted rakishly over one ear, Nancy came fighting her way down Saint Louis Street and across the Place d'Armes. Her pulses were pounding gayly with the intoxication of the cold; her face glowed with the struggle of meeting the boisterous wind. From his ducal casement, Barth eyed her wishfully. Then he returned to his book. Nancy, in such a mood as that, defied his powers of comprehension. Upon one former occasion he had seen her thus, a veritable spirit of the storm. Experience had taught him certain lessons. Mr. Cecil Barth looked down on Nancy's erect head and blazing cheeks, on her vigorous, elastic tread. Looking, he sighed, and prudently remained hidden in his room.

Ten minutes later, Nancy's shut hand descended upon her father's door. The door was locked.

"Oh, daddy, are you there?" she called ingratiatingly.

There was no reply, and she tapped again. This time, the doctor answered.

"Busy, Nancy."

"Really and truly?" she wheedled.

"Yes."

"Oh, how mean of you! How long?"

"I can't tell."

Her lips to the keyhole, she heaved an ostentatious sigh. The sigh brought forth no sign of relenting.

"I am very lonesome, daddy," she said then. "It is too bad of you to neglect me like this. But, if you really won't let me in, I'm going out on the ramparts for a breath of fresh air."

"Well," the doctor's accent bespoke his manifest relief. "Go on, dear; but don't get blown away."

"No; and don't you fall asleep over your horrid old manuscripts, and forget to let yourself out and come down to supper," she cautioned him. "Good by."

Going back to her room, she took off her jacket and broad hat, and replaced them with a sealskin coat and toque. Then she went running down the stairs and turned out into Sainte Anne Street, already powdered thickly with falling flakes.

With the coming of the snow, the wind was dying, and Nancy made her way easily enough around the corner into Buade Street, past the Chien d'Or, gnawing his perennial bone high in the air, and out to the northeast corner of the city wall where she halted, breathless, beside one of the venerable guns.

Just then, the door of the doctor's room opened, and Adolphe St. Jacques stepped out into the hall.

"Courage, boy!" said the doctor kindly.

And St. Jacques nodded in silence, as he gripped the outstretched hand.

As a matter of course, he took his way straight in the direction of the ramparts. St. Jacques could think of but one person in the world, just then; and that person was Nancy Howard. He overtook her at the angle of the ancient wall. Later, it occurred to him that there was a symbolic meaning in the situation, as he came hurrying onward, with Laval at his left, Nancy at his right, and the brief, empty stretch of road before him. At the time, however, he had but one thought, and that was to get to Nancy.

He found her standing with her back towards the direction from whence he came. One arm lay lightly across the cannon, the other rested on the old gray parapet which made a fitting background for her slight figure in its dark cloth skirt and dark fur coat. Her shoulders were sprinkled with the fine, soft snow and, against the snowy air above the river, her vivid hair, loosened by the wind, stood out in a gleaming aureole above the high collar of her coat.

"Miss Howard!"

She turned with a start to find St. Jacques at her side. Releasing the cannon, she held out her hand in blithe greeting.

"Isn't this superb?" she exclaimed breathlessly. "I am so glad you have come to enjoy it with me. See how the river is all blown into a chopping sea! And the snow over Lévis! And look at those thick clouds of snow that keep scurrying across the river! How can people stay in-doors and lose it all?"

For an instant, St. Jacques felt himself dazzled by her beauty and by her strong vitality. In all his past experience, there had been no other Nancy. He sought to get a firm grasp upon himself. The instant's delay caught Nancy's quick attention, and she shrank from him, as she saw his rigid face and lambent eyes. Then she rallied and laughed lightly.

"What is it, M. St. Jacques?" she queried. "You look as if you had seen a ghost."

"So I have."

"Was it a pretty one?" she asked nervously, as she locked her hands above the crowned monogram on the gun, and stood looking at him a little defiantly.

He shook his head.

"It was the ghost of what I might have been," he answered quietly.

Again Nancy sought to dominate the scene.

"So bad as that?" she asked, with a futile attempt at flippancy.

He disregarded her words.

"Miss Howard," he said slowly; "I have come to say good by."

Instantly her tone changed.

"Oh, I am so sorry! Is it for a long time?"

"I may not come back while you are here."

It was plain that he was struggling hard to hold himself steady; and Nancy, at a loss to explain the situation, nevertheless found herself sharing his mood.

"I am sorry," she repeated slowly. "Are you going to leave Quebec?"

"I am going home."

"There is no trouble there, I hope."

"No. The trouble is all here."

Nancy's mind went swiftly southward to the frisky, boyish days that unfold themselves at Yale.

"At Laval?" she questioned, with a smile.

St. Jacques shook his head.

"What should be the trouble at Laval?" he asked.

"Oh, nothing; unless you have come into collision with a dean or two," she answered hastily.

St. Jacques smiled, with a pitiful attempt at mirth.

"No. On the other hand, something came into collision with me."

"What was that?"

For his only answer, he brushed aside his hair and let the storm sweep pitilessly against the scar beneath. Nancy caught her breath sharply.

"M. St. Jacques! Do you mean that it is going to be serious?"

"So serious that I must give up all work."

"Who says so?" she demanded.

"Your father."

"My father?" Nancy's accent dropped to utter hopelessness. "For how long?"

"Until I am better."

"And when will that be?"

"He says it is impossible for him to tell. Perhaps—"

"Perhaps?" Nancy echoed questioningly.

"Perhaps—never."

There was no answer for a moment. Then Nancy's glove tore itself across with the strain of her clenched fingers.

"Oh, I could kill the man who struck that blow!" she burst out. Then her head went down on the crowned monogram, and the silence dropped again.

At length, Nancy raised her head.

"Shall we walk on?" she asked, as steadily as she could. "It is very cold here, all at once."

Side by side, they turned the corner to the westward, and came into comparative shelter.

"How long have you known it?" she said, as soon as she could speak quietly.

"Just as you came to the door of your father's room."

She drew a slow breath, as she looked up at his face, white, but resolute still.

"And already it seems ages old. You are sure?"

"He is. It has been coming on for a month now. Three weeks ago, I went to your father and told him that I feared there was trouble. He bade me wait, to live out of doors and to work as little as possible. I kept the hope. My profession means so much to me now, that I could not give it up."

"Yes, I know. Your profession is your very life," Nancy answered gently.

Swiftly he turned and faced her. In that one glance, Nancy saw all the fiery, repressed nature of the man, read his secret and, with a sinking heart, acknowledged to herself the fatal keenness of the blow which she must one day in honor deal.

But the answer of St. Jacques was already in her ears.

"It means far more than life."

She tried to stem the tide of his words.

"When do you go?" she asked hurriedly.

"To-morrow."

"So soon as that?"

"There must be an operation."

"Where?"

"At my home. Your father will go with me. Every one says no greater man can be found. He is very good," St. Jacques added simply.

Again Nancy's courage failed her. Again she looked into her companion's face, and took heart from the resolution written there.

"I wish I knew what to say," she said quietly.

"Sometimes there is nothing to say. It is all said for us," he replied, with sudden dreariness. "Meanwhile, may I ask a favor of you?"

"Of course."

"You have your little Sainte Anne?"

For her only answer, she took it from the folds of her blouse and laid it in his hand. He walked on for a moment, looking down at it with loving, reverent eyes. Then he gave it back into her keeping.

"I had hoped so much from it," he said slowly; "so much more than you ever knew. I regarded the name as an omen of good. I even made my novena; but it was all in vain." His voice dropped. "All in vain." Then he steadied himself. "But the favor? It is to be next Thursday, three days from now. The operation, I mean. On that day, will you go out to the shrine of the Good Sainte Anne, and say a prayer for me? You are no Catholic, I know; but it will help me to be brave, if I can feel that together you and she are making intercession in my behalf."

Resolutely Nancy brushed the tears from her cheeks and faced him with a smile.

"I—promise," she said. Then her voice failed her again.

"Thank you. It will be a help. Beyond that, I ask nothing of you. In the one case, it could do no good. In the other, I shall come back to you. There is no need to tell you all I have wished—and hoped—and prayed for, all you have been in my life, these past weeks. If the Good Sainte Anne wills it, I shall tell it all to you, some day. If not—good by."

As he took her hand into his strong fingers, Nancy's tear-dim eyes were blind to everything but the unspoken love and longing in the great dark eyes before her, everything but the point of the lower lip rolling outward in its pitiful attempt to form its own brave, characteristic little smile.

Then, hat in hand and the snow sifting down on his thick dark hair, he turned away and left her alone beside the old gray wall in the fast-gathering snow.

CHAPTER TWENTY-THREE

Five days later, the doctor came back from Rimouski. Nancy, on the platform of the station, waited eagerly until he came in sight. Then she stepped back and hid her face.

"It was all so like his life," her father said, when they sat together in his room, that night; "brave and quiet and full of thought for us all. Once he rallied for a few hours, and we felt there was hope. At the very last, he gave me this for you. He said you would understand." And the doctor laid in Nancy's palm a tiny figure of the Good Sainte Anne, the exact duplicate of her own, save that its silver base bore the arms of St. Jacques and, beneath, two plain initials: *N* and *H*.

A week later, Nancy rose from her knees beside her father's open trunk, and stood staring down into the courtyard. Wrapped to his ears, the old habitant still sat on his block in the corner, peeling potatoes without end. Far above his head, a stray shaft of sunshine gilded the gray wall and reminded Nancy of her resolution to take a final walk, that morning.

It was almost with a feeling of relief that Nancy saw the approaching end of her stay at The Maple Leaf. The past days had held some of the saddest hours she had ever known. Till then, she had never realized how the bright, brave personality of the sturdy little Frenchman had pervaded the place, how acutely she could mourn for a man of whom, less than six weeks before, she had never even heard. Forget him she could not. She and Brock talked of him by the hour, now laughing over the merry days they had spent together, then giving up to the sudden wave of loneliness which swept over them at the thought of the *nevermore* that separated them from their good comrade. As yet, it was too soon for them to take comfort from the doctor's words, that the swift passing of Adolphe St. Jacques had been but the merciful forestalling of a pitiful, lingering death in life.

To one day, Nancy never made any allusion. That was the day she had spent alone, at the shrine of the Good Sainte Anne.

Now, as she stood before her mirror, fastening on her hat, her glance fell to the little figure of the good saint and, taking it up, she looked long at the symbols graven on its base. She hesitated. Then she gently slid it into the breast pocket of her coat. In loyalty to St. Jacques, it still should be her companion. His eyes now, in the clearer light, could see what had before been hidden from them. Adolphe St. Jacques was too unselfishly loyal to fail to understand the nature of the only love she could ever have given him and, understanding, to reject it.

Inside the city wall, the early snow had vanished; but it still lay white over the Cove Fields, over the ruins of the old French fortifications, and over the plains beyond. Beyond Saint Sauveur, the hills were blue in the sunshine, and the light wind that swept in from their snowy caps, was crisp and full of ozone. Nancy had left The Maple Leaf with slow step and drooping head; she went tramping along the Grand Allée as if the world were all before her, to be had for the mere sake of asking. Then, as she turned again and halted by the Wolfe monument, her buoyant mood forsook her. That simple shaft marked the end of one who died, victorious. It spoke no word of those others, Frenchmen, brave, true-hearted fellows who fell there in their hour of defeat. And not one of them was braver, more true-hearted than little Adolphe St. Jacques.

"Oh, Miss Howard."

Impatiently she raised her head from the cold iron palings. Barth was standing close at her side. Even as she nodded to him, she felt a sudden shrinking from his inevitable question as to the cause for her tears. To her surprise, no question came.

"After all, he was a wonderfully good little fellow," Barth said simply.

She nodded, without speaking. Barth let full five minutes pass, before he spoke again.

"I saw you go by the house," he said then. "I fancied you would come out here. I knew you liked the place."

"Yes."

"And so I followed you. I wanted to see you, if I could. Miss Howard, I shall miss you."

"I am glad of that. It would be dreary to feel that no one mourned for our departure."

"Oh, yes," Barth agreed. "Shall we go on for a little walk?"

With one last look at the shaft and its deathless words, Nancy turned and followed him back to the Grand Allée, back from the place of the dead to the haunts of the living.

"Do you go, to-morrow?" Barth asked, after another pause.

"To-morrow noon."

"It is going to be very lonely," he said.

"I am glad," she repeated.

Even to Barth's conservative mind, the conversation did not appear to be making much progress. He turned and peered into Nancy's thoughtful face.

"Oh, Miss Howard, would you be willing to give me your address?" he asked abruptly.

"Of course, if you wish it," she assented cordially.

"Rather! I might call on you, you know, if I ever went to The States."

"That would be delightful. So you think you will come across the border?"

"Perhaps. I have often wondered, just lately, you know, what I would think of The States. What do you think?"

"That I love them," Nancy said loyally.

"Oh, yes. But what do you think that I would think?"

Nancy laughed outright, as she met his anxious eyes.

"That it is never safe to predict. I advise you to come and see for yourself."

Barth's face cleared.

"Thank you, you know. And the address?"

"I haven't any cards here."

"Oh, but I have." And Barth hastily took out his cardcase. Then, with infinite difficulty, he focussed upon a card the tip of the little gold pencil that dangled from his watchchain.

Nancy dictated the address. Then she laughed.

"The idea of tying your pencil to you!" she commented irreverently.

"Why not? Then one doesn't lose it, you know."

"Yes, I do know. It reminds me of the way I used to have my mittens sewed to the ends of a piece of braid," Nancy responded.

Barth looked up from his half-written card.

"Really? How interesting! But, Miss Howard—" He halted abruptly.

"What now?"

"About The States. You feel they are the only place to live in?"

"Certainly," Nancy replied promptly.

"Oh. Have you ever been to England?"

"No." Nancy began to wonder at the antiquity of British customs. At this rate of progress, it would take aeons for a Britisher to evolve a custom of any sort. Already her mind had outstripped the deliberate mental processes of Barth. She also began to wonder impatiently how long it would take him to come to the point. There seemed to her something inhuman in allowing him to remain on the rack of suspense. Nevertheless, she felt that it would be altogether unseemly for her to refuse anything before she was asked.

"Don't you want to go to England?" Barth continued calmly.

"Yes, of course. I want to visit it. However, that doesn't mean that I wish to take up my abode there."

"Oh. I am sorry. Still," Barth went on meditatively; "I dare say one could make out very well, even if he had to live in The States."

"I certainly expect to," Nancy responded coolly.

Again he peered into her face.

"Oh; but I don't refer to you," he said hastily. "I was speaking of myself."

"But I thought you were going out to a ranch."

"That was before I met you," Barth answered, with quiet directness.

Suddenly a change came over him. Throwing back his shoulders, he faced Nancy with a resolution which brought new lustre to his eyes, new lines of character into his boyish face. And Nancy, as she saw the change in him, trembled for the decision which, with infinite difficulty, she had long been fixing in her girlish mind.

"Miss Howard," he asked abruptly; "do you believe in the Good Sainte Anne?"

Without speaking, Nancy let her hand rest lightly on the little silver image in the pocket of her coat. Then she nodded in silence.

"So do I," Barth answered. "I am not a Catholic; still, I believe that the good lady has had me in her keeping, and I trust she may continue her care for me. Miss Howard, I am English; you are American, very American indeed. However, different as we are, I think our lives need each other. I had never thought," he hesitated; then, cap in hand, he stood looking directly into her blushing face; "I had never supposed that my life could hold a love like what has grown into it. I dare not face that life without—Miss Howard," he added, with a swift change to the simple boyishness which became him so well; "my life is all yours, to do what you like with. I shall try to meet your decision bravely; but I do hope you won't throw me to one side, as of no use."

But Nancy walked on without answering; and Barth, still cap in hand, moved on at her side.

"It began a long while ago," he added at length. "I really think it must have started, that day at the shrine of Sainte Anne."

Again Nancy's hand caressed the little image in her pocket.

"I think perhaps it did," she assented.

For a moment, Barth walked on in silence, unable to construe her words into the phrase which he was waiting to hear. Then he spoke again.

"I went out to Sainte Anne-de-Beaupré, one morning last week," he said slowly. "It was very desolate there, at this season. I walked out on the pier. Then I went back and sat in the church for quite a long time, and I thought about things. Miss Howard, I wish I had never given you that guinea."

With an odd little laugh, which was yet half a sob, Nancy put her hand into her pocket, felt about underneath the little silver image, and slowly drew out a shining bit of gold.

"Here it is, Mr. Barth," she said. "Take it back, if you wish it."

Taking it from her outstretched hand, he stared at it intently for a moment. Then he held it out to her again.

"And you have carried it, all this time?"

"No," she confessed reluctantly. "Only lately."

"Oh, but—"

"I have called it my lucky penny," she interrupted, with a smile. "I had never supposed you would regret giving it to me."

Still with the coin in the hollow of his hand, he put on his glasses and peered into her face. He read there something which he had missed in her tone. Dropping his glasses again, he held out the shining golden guinea.

"Please take it back again," he said, and in his voice there came a sudden imperious accent which was new to Nancy. "And, when you take it, take me, too. We both are yours, you know."

The girl moved steadily on for a step or two, her eyes fixed upon the strip of path before her. Then her step lagged a little and, turning, she smiled up into Barth's troubled, waiting eyes, while she held out her hand for the coin.

"Give it back to me, then," she said quietly. "It is mine."

"With all it must mean,—Nancy?"

"Yes. With all it does mean."

Their hands met about the shining piece of gold, and it was an instant before they dropped apart again. Then Barth gave a contented little sigh.

"And now," he said slowly; "now at last I really can call you my Good Sainte Anne. Oh, rather!"

Milton Keynes UK
Ingram Content Group UK Ltd.
UKHW022152250224
438379UK00006B/724